It's a Match

Match
(Cocktails for You)

Susanne Matthews

PUBLISHER

MHSLM

COVER ART
Melinda De Ross

ISBN: 9798867794422

Book Description

They were a perfect match—until she caught him with another woman. When Marissa canceled the wedding and left her hometown, she refused to listen to Zak's excuses. Now, five years later, she's in the UK for her sister's wedding and so is he, determined to set the record straight.

Marissa Kimble had everything she'd ever wanted—a promising career as an electrician and Zak Mitchum, the man she adored, had just proposed. What more could she possibly want?

But fate is a cruel mistress. Everything went wrong when she walked in on Zak and Karen in a hot tub. It was hard to mistake what was happening for anything but what it was. With her trust destroyed, her heart broken, and her pride in shreds, Marissa escaped from Cedar Lake, leaving everything behind, searching for a place to lick her wounds.

Discovering her sister was marrying into royalty and wanted her to be the Maid of Honor was both exciting and terrifying. Not only was she a first-class klutz without any experience in the world of the rich and famous, but her sister also conveniently forgot to mention that Zak would be there, as well as Karen and a few others who'd made growing up in Cedar Lake miserable. As hard as Marissa's tried, she can't forgive or forget either of them. Zak is determined that she hears his side of the story, but will she listen?

To further complicate matters, Ken, Karen's brother, is determined to get her to see him as more than an old tormentor. Will she succumb to his temptation, or will she forgive Zak and give them another chance? Love is often more complicated the second time around.

Praise for Other Books in this Series

A fun, playful chick lit with super cute characters and sassy dialogue. One of those books that's perfect to read anywhere, anytime! (Tequila Sunrise)

I enjoyed this story. Even the animals were full of personality. Romance lovers and animal lovers will be entertained by this tale of triumph. (The Tipsy Pig)

Enjoyable easy, breezy read. I laughed aloud more than once, learned about some alcoholic beverages, and had a nice escape from everyday life following Savannah on her journey to New York. Luke was just the "cherry" on top! (Make Mine a Manhattan)

CONTENTS

"Sometimes you were handed a second chance, and all you had to do was close your eyes and step into it."

Jean Oram

CHAPTER ONE

"You don't have to pick me up tonight, Rissa," Zak said, slipping his arms into one of the plaid shirts he loved. "Go home after work. I'll call you when I crawl out of bed."

I sometimes spent the night at his apartment instead of going home. With Mom and Dad out of town this week, it was easier than ever, and I didn't have to hear Dad's 'if you give away the milk, no one's going to want to buy the cow' speech, although since we'd officially become engaged last month, he'd eased up on it. I loved my folks, but they hadn't quite made it into the twenty-first century.

"I told you, I don't mind, and since I plan to be here anyway..."

"It'll be late. You've had a long week, and you're putting in overtime today. Just go to bed, and I'll tell you all about it in the morning." He chuckled. "With Ken in charge of things, it'll probably just be one massive beer pong tournament and one drinking game after another. He still sees himself as a frat boy. I can take a cab home."

I smiled. How I loved this guy. Always thinking of others. Here he was offering to give me sack time and not put me out when all I wanted was to stretch out beside him once more and make love.

"Are you kidding? I know how sappy you get when you've had too much to drink." I giggled. "I don't want you giving any of that sweetness to anyone but me. I'll be there at midnight, ready to pour you into the van, and then tuck you into bed."

He pulled me into his arms, his bare chest rubbing against mine. "And is all you want to do tuck me in?"

My nipples hardened against him. No matter how many times we made love, I was always ready, willing, and able to go at it again.

"Maybe I'll be up for something more—if you're in shape to oblige," I whispered, feeling him harden against me. I wasn't what you might call adventurous in bed, but I was learning.

"I'm always up for you."

He bent his head and captured my lips in one of his soul-searing kisses, the kind that turned me into mush. I reciprocated with everything in me, my tongue dueling with his, my mouth filling with the taste of him, kindling a fire in my belly. How was it possible that the mere meeting of lips and the tender touch of tongues could generate such wanton desire?

Slowly, he pulled away. "Marissa Kimble, I'd love nothing more than to take you back to bed and spend the entire day making love to you, but we both have to get to work." He smacked my butt lightly. "But one of these days, I plan to do just that. I'm closing the clinic at two. Ken's going to pick me up on his way by, and we'll grab the last of the food and drink before heading back to his place. The rest of the guys will get there around four."

I rolled my eyes. Knowing Ken and his penchant for the ladies, after the monster steak barbecue, there would probably be a stripper or two dropping by as well. The man had class—all of it at the scummiest level possible. He never failed to live down to my lowest expectations of him. Why Zak and he were friends was beyond me, but then while I might work in a male-dominated profession, I didn't think like one. I'd learned to ignore the blonde jokes, dress not to attract attention, and do the work to the best of my abilities. It had taken time, but I'd earned the respect of my coworkers. I loved what I did, was good at it, and they knew it.

I smiled and punched Zak's shoulder. "Don't act as if this is such a chore for you, Zak Mitchum. I can see right through you. You're as excited about this party for Nate Miller as every other guy in town. Cedar Lake's very own playing professional hockey in Europe. It's a big deal, and we both know it. I'm sure you'll have fun—but don't have too much fun, okay? I'll pick you up at midnight. Almost ten hours of alcohol consumption should be more than enough for you! Don't forget, hungover or not, you have to put in an appearance at your grandmother's ninetieth birthday party tomorrow. I can do the driving, but it's going to be a long day if you've got a headache, upset stomach, and shakes. You can be damn sure your teetotalling aunt won't be too sympathetic either."

"That's why I love you, Rissa. You've always got my back. You're there when I need you, and you'll never let me down. Now, I've got to boogie, or I'll be late. Mrs. Swanson's cat should be ready to go home this morning, and I know she'll be there to pick him up as soon as the door opens." He hurried to dress. Grabbing his keys off the dresser, he kissed me quickly. "See you tonight." Then, he was gone.

Reluctantly, I headed into the bathroom to get ready for the day. We were rewiring an old ski lodge in the Foothills. While the job should only take five or six hours, working in old buildings often took a lot more. You never knew what you were up against until you got there. They were taking down the inside walls today. All I could do was hope that Mother Nature hadn't left us too many surprises.

* * *

By eleven o'clock that night, there was nothing I wanted more than my bed. If something could go wrong on a job, it had, and we'd run wire three times before finally getting it the way we wanted it. I'd skipped lunch and dinner, and now, even though I was hungry, I didn't dare eat. A plateful of carbs would have me face down on the table. I'd called Zak to suggest he take that cab, but his phone had gone straight to voice mail, so here I was keeping a promise I wished I'd never made.

While the Atchison house was only twenty minutes from downtown, I needed to be awake and alert to drive there. Country roads were notoriously dark, especially when there was no light in the sky, thanks to the new moon. At this time of year, the deer were active at night, and even in my work van, hitting a deer could prove fatal for both the animal and myself.

I pulled up in front of the Atchison house at eleven-forty-five, hoping I wouldn't have to wait too long for Zak. Ken Atchison and his twin sister, Karen, had been pains in my ass ever since the minute they'd been born, approximately thirty minutes after me. The preemies had required so much attention that Mom had chosen to take me home from the hospital early rather than deal with all that drama. Since Cedar Lake was a small community, the three of us had grown up, doing everything kids do together—always together. We attended the same school, played the same sports, joined the same clubs, and participated in the same activities. Hell, we even shared birthday parties ... after all, there were only so many kids in town.

Given all of that, you would probably expect us to be close. Nothing could be farther from the truth.

While on the surface we were friends, there was always an undercurrent of *je ne sais quoi*—jealousy, envy, or maybe just plain hatred. Who knew? But whatever it was, it was always there, lurking under a fake smile or masquerading under our competitive edges.

The fact that, as children, the three of us resembled each other since our mothers were second cousins hadn't helped. On more than one occasion, I'd been mistaken for Karen and dragged into the principal's office for something I hadn't done, or she'd received accolades for something I'd done instead of her. It might've been fun if she hadn't been such a prissy prima donna while I had no use for frills and lace. When people saw the three of us together for the first time, they found it hard to believe that we weren't triplets. Thankfully, as we'd aged, the similarities had decreased. Ken and Karen's blond hair had turned dark, while mine had remained flaxen. As well, their eyes were green, while mine were a clear, sapphire blue, and finally, while I'd grown buxomer than I liked,

Karen had remained thin, gangly, and small-breasted, which had added to my misery since her fat jokes and those of her despicable friends, Billie and April, always hit the mark. The titties Karen had acquired in Calgary when she finished university had probably cost her a small fortune.

Even though we'd all embraced different careers—Karen was a trauma nurse, Ken a chemical engineer, and I'd become an electrician—we still lived and worked in Cedar Lake and competed for everything and anything from the annual half-marathon for charity, always coming in first, second, and third, but not necessarily in the same order, to fundraising for one service organization or another. It seemed that it had always been a case of what one had, the others wanted. We might not all be siblings, but the rivalry was there, and getting older hadn't made it any more bearable.

All through high school, Karen and I had competed for the attention of the same guys, too, until our final year when Zak Mitchum moved to town. He'd taken over as captain of the football team, and he'd chosen me over my doppelganger right from the start, something that had annoyed the hell out of her even if she behaved as if it didn't matter.

I'd seen the scheming look in her eyes when he'd gone to university in Calgary—the same place she and Ken had chosen—while I'd stayed behind to start my apprenticeship. We might not have said the words, but Zak was mine. He called almost every night and came home one weekend a month, often sharing a ride with Ken who still called me the Ice Queen because I tended to ignore him, which only pissed him off more.

When Zak graduated with his degree in veterinary medicine, he returned to Cedar Lake and joined Dr. Ingles's clinic. Now, two years later, he'd popped the question and we would be married in October. By this time next year, I hoped to be pregnant. Great job, husband, house, and baby. What more could I possibly want?

I glanced over at the two-story house. When their parents decided to move to the Vancouver area and warmer weather, Ken and Karen had taken over the family home, sharing its costs and maintenance. The first to marry would have dibs on the house. Since the place had a separate apartment, there would be no need to leave until they were good and ready. Knowing Ken's reputation as a love 'em and leave 'em kind of guy, I expected Karen would eventually get the house ... not that I cared one way or another. Zak and I were looking at smaller bungalows in town, the kind with slightly larger than a postage stamp lawn that would require little maintenance since we both had black thumbs rather than green ones. If it were possible to kill an artificial plant, I could probably do it. There was a house over on Sycamore Circle that I adored. It was a little pricy, but with both of us working, we could probably manage it.

I yawned and glanced around. The first thing that penetrated my tired brain was the lack of cars in the driveway. While I would like to believe everyone was mature enough not to drink and drive, the reality was quite the opposite, and even if they had chosen not to drive drunk, wouldn't at least one of them have driven here tonight?

The second thing was how quiet it was. There were a few lights on in the house, but the only sounds belonged to crickets, frogs, and the whistle of a freight train in the distance. I checked my watch. Midnight. Right on time. I got out of the van and went up to the front door. I rang the bell and waited. No one answered.

The hoot of an owl sent goosebumps racing down my spine. I recalled a book I'd read in high school about owls and premonitions of death and sorrow.

Where the hell was everyone? Had the place been raided and all of them carted off to jail? It would serve them right—at least Ken. If anyone skirted the letter of the law, it was him. He called it living on the edge; I called it stupid and irresponsible.

I stopped walking to check my phone for messages. None.

Going around the house, I heard soft music coming from the pool area. Maybe they'd all passed out early. They weren't spring chickens any longer. Unfortunately, alcohol had a way of making even the young feel aged. I reached over the top and unbolted the gate, letting myself into the yard.

Over the sounds of Blue Rodeo, I could hear the bubbling of the hot tub. The yard was littered with red and blue Solo cups and beer cans, proof that there had been one hell of a party here. I turned the corner and stopped cold. The pool deck and patio were deserted, but not so the spa area.

A woman, naked at least from the waist up, her long, wet hair streaming down her back was kneeling in front of a naked man sitting on the edge of the tub, his back against the wall, his head thrown back, his eyes closed, his ... I started to back away until the bells and whistles exploded inside my addled mind, and I recognized the mole on the man's shoulder.

"Zak!" The word exploded from me.

He opened his gray eyes, blinked, and smiled. The woman stopped what she was doing and turned to look at me. Karen.

"What the hell do you think you're doing?" I screamed.

She giggled. "I would think that was obvious."

Zak's eyes opened wider and his forehead creased. "Rissa? What are you doing over there?"

The door into the house slid open. "What's all the yelling about?" Ken took in the scene. "Oh shit! Karen, for God's sake, put something on."

Standing tall, hurt beyond words, but refusing to give in to the pain, I stood my ground, adopting the same lackadaisical tone I had every single time Karen or Ken had outshined me. If ever there was a time to go into Ice Queen mode, this was it.

"It's okay. I'm just leaving. It seems Zak isn't quite ready to go." I might be pretending to be fine, but the fury in my voice was unmistakable.

"Lighten up, Rissa, for God's sake," Ken said, slurring his words, proof that he too was drunk. "It's only a blow job. You two aren't married yet, and despite his desire to shackle himself to the Ice Queen, he does have some heat running through his veins and other places. Maybe he wanted a warm woman for a change instead of one determined to wear the pants in the relationship. I, on the other hand, am open to experimenting."

"Not with me. Allow me to make it easier on him and your sister." I pulled off my engagement ring and threw it at the couple in the tub, the platinum and diamond ring scarcely making a sound as it plopped into the bubbling water. "If she wants him, she can have him. This Ice Queen is out of here. All of you can enjoy what's left of the party." I almost choked on the last word, the tears filling my throat, keeping the bile from my stomach in place.

Turning around and walking with all the decorum I could manage, ignoring Zak's "Rissa, where are you going?" question, I went back to my van, started the engine, and backed out of the laneway. The next thing I knew, I was pulling into the driveway at home.

I let myself into the house and went up to my room. Without skipping a beat, I packed my clothing, toiletries, documentation, and other things I couldn't bear to leave behind. I turned off my cell phone, removed the SIM card, and flushed it down the toilet. Zak was bound to call, and when he did, he wouldn't get hold of me. No one would. There was nothing any of them could ever say that would make this right. I shoved the useless device into my messenger bag. I wrote a note to my parents and another to my employer that I asked Mom to deliver. Without giving any details, I told them that my engagement was off and that while they wouldn't be able to reach me, I would contact them once I was settled, assuring them that I was fine and needed a change of scenery.

Two hours later, with a full tank of gas, I was on the highway heading east. Where was I going? I had no idea, but I couldn't stay in Cedar Lake. There was no way I could ever face Zak, Ken, or Karen again. No wonder he hadn't wanted me to pick him up. Dad's comment about free milk might've been right after all. Once more, I'd come in second place to Karen, but never again.

It was almost noon when I pulled into the parking lot of a small motel outside of Moose Jaw, Saskatchewan.

I checked into the place, paid for two nights' accommodations, and then dragged what I would need out of the car. Once inside the room, I collapsed onto the bed and gave in to all the pain and misery within me.

All of my hopes and dreams had been shattered in the cruelest way possible. I might want to die, but that would be taking the easy way out for me. It would crush Mom, Dad, and Marley. No. I would move on from this, redefine myself, grow another backbone, and make a new life for myself ... I'd done it before, competing in a man's world for the job I wanted. I would do it again. Where? I didn't know, but it would be as far away from Cedar Lake as I could get.

* * *

Five years later

Have you ever had that waiting for the other shoe to drop feeling? That dark cloud hanging over you when everyone else was looking at sunshine and roses? That was how I felt this morning. Could it be the date? Today was the fifth anniversary of the worst day of my life. The first one had been tough, but the others had passed with scarcely a tear. Perhaps it was because I was all but exhausted, thanks to too little sleep this week.

So far, everything was going according to plan, but as I'd learned the hard way, plans couldn't be trusted. The day was young. Anything could go wrong. I'd slept through the night without a single one of *those* dreams, getting up on time, showering without getting soap or shampoo in my eyes, and managing to finish my first cup of coffee while it was still warm. I'd even fed Frodo before he started mewling over my neglect.

I'd found the kitten shivering in the rain in an alleyway in Thunder Bay, and knowing how it felt to be abandoned by the one you loved, I picked him up in my sweater and put him inside the car. I was going to drop him off at the local animal shelter, but one look into his innocent blue eyes, and I changed my mind. Dewormed, with all his shots, new cat cage, cat bed, and a bazillion other things he just had to have, we'd continued on our way east. Now, the cat was my sole companion. He and I were inseparable.

Once he'd settled in front of his bowls for breakfast, I'd scarfed down two slices of cold pizza, not necessarily my best meal choice, but with the unexpected heat spell, I'd been putting in twelve-hour days all week. I barely had the energy to eat anything before collapsing into bed. Thank God tomorrow was Sunday. Everyone deserved a day off work.

The apartment was more or less tidy. I'd managed to get rid of the stench of dirty feet from my work boots when I'd accidentally removed them in the apartment instead of the shop, and had vacuumed up enough cat hair to knit another cat. I would never win an award for Housekeeper of the Year, but hey, I had no one to impress but myself. With Frodo asleep in the center of my bed, I'd gone down to the shop, hoping to pack up the van and be on the road as soon as Bridget, my Girl Friday who handled the shop and the phone, arrived. I'd penciled in a lunch and dinner break into my schedule today, so why was I so antsy? Maybe because everything was going so well ... why was I tempting fate by questioning it?

Five years ago, the water pump on my work van on its last legs, I'd gotten off the main highway, following the lesser country roads, looking for a small town with a garage that might help. I'd found Brockton, population 12,359. After settling into a second-rate motel, I left Frodo in the room with his bowls newly filled and drove the van to *Smitty's Garage*. Satisfied that he'd be able to get the van up and running the following day, I went looking for something to eat. I'd only gone a block or so when I spotted *Callaghan's* across the street. I was about to cross when I noticed the sign in the window beside me. **Wanted Immediately. Certified Electrician.**

I can't say what prompted me to open the door and go inside since I had no plans to stay in the town that reminded me of home, but when I walked in and saw Mr. Porter sitting there with his leg in a cast, I knew I had to do something to help. The poor man, the only electrician in town, had fallen off a ladder. He'd put up the sign that morning, praying God would send help. He saw my arrival as Divine Intervention. Maybe it was. I'd been on the road for a month and I was ready to stop running.

He'd checked my credentials and had hired me on the spot. A year and a half later, using the money I'd inherited from my grandmother, I bought the building and the business from him. He dropped by now and then to chew the fat, and occasionally helped me out if I had a big job, or when I opted to take time off—not that I had in months.

I'd barely unlocked the door when my first customer arrived, not that I wanted to make sales when I needed to get ready to go out to the various job sites I already had booked for the day, but three hundred and seventy bucks were worth a minor delay. I depressed the keys. The cash register dinged as the drawer opened. I waited for the debit sale to process, tore off my copy, and put it in the cash drawer.

"There you go, Mrs. Wendel." I handed the woman her receipt for the ceiling fan she'd just purchased, installation included. "I'll bring it with me at one when I come to install it for you."

So what if that penciled-in lunch break had just vanished? I'd grab something when I needed it, just as I had yesterday. Maybe pizza for breakfast hadn't been a bad choice after all, and if this were to be the only snag in my day, I could live with it.

"Bless you, Marissa. I meant to get that fixed before the heat came, but..." She shrugged.

I chuckled. "Thirty degrees Celsius in May caught us all by surprise. You'll sleep comfortably tonight, I promise."

Regina Wendel, wife of the mayor and probably the most important woman in Brockton, waved at me as she exited the shop, the tiny bell at the top of the door tinkling its farewell note. When I bought the business, it was her support that got me the clients I needed to start. I would like to think that my reputation was doing it for me now, but it never hurt to have powerful people on your side.

In a lot of ways, Regina reminded me of my mother. No matter the time of day or the weather outside, she looked as if she'd stepped off the cover of *Vogue*, her silver hair styled, her makeup applied just right, and her clothing as perfect and fashionable as it came. I, on the other hand, usually looked like something the cat had dragged in, no cosmetics, my fair hair in a ponytail, and dressed in baggy, stained, gray overalls. I couldn't tell you what some of those marks all over my work clothes were if my life depended on it, but I was certain grease and chocolate had to be there somewhere. Mom might be disappointed that I hadn't turned into the girly girl she'd always wanted, but she loved and supported me ... and worried about me more than she should.

A wave of nostalgia flowed over me. I hadn't been back to Cedar Lake since I'd left. I'd met Mom, Dad, and Marley in Ottawa at Christmas, but that seemed like ages ago. Come to think of it, it had been three years ago, just before COVID. I'd seen Mom and Dad since then, meeting them in Niagara Falls once and Toronto at least twice, but COVID had kept us apart making it easier and normalizing meeting over the Internet rather than in person. Going home now would be pointless since Mom and Dad were on the first leg of an extended European vacation and wouldn't be back until mid-September. Believe me. There was no one else in that town that I wanted to see.

I glanced at my watch. Eight fifteen a.m. My first installation was set for nine fifteen, which gave me time to check inventory and do the countless other things I had to do as the electrician and owner. The only reason I was still here was that Bridget wasn't in yet. She had to drop Oli, her four-year-old, off at school. I don't know how I would have managed to succeed in this business without her.

Reasonably new in town and trying to maintain the company's goodwill, I needed part-time help. Bridget had shown up with the baby carriage, looking too tired and depressed for words. My heart had gone out to her. Since I'd had great dreams of having a child of my own back then, I'd caved in and hired the single mother, allowing her to keep the baby at work with her. When Oli outgrew the playpen, she registered him in daycare, and now the boy attended full-day kindergarten.

Bridget answered the phone, booked appointments for me, and made the odd sale. We needed each other. She'd been dumped by her worthless boyfriend who wasn't ready to be a father, and I'd been dumped by one who wasn't ready to be faithful. Two women on our own, fighting for ourselves. It was a match made in heaven.

I sighed. A match made in heaven? How ironic. I thought I'd found my perfect match which had turned into a perfect nightmare. At least, Mom wouldn't be calling me to commiserate this year. I'd never breathed a single word about what had happened and surprisingly, neither Ken nor Karen had let that particular cat out of the bag. They'd allowed me to keep my basic dignity, so maybe they did have a gram of decency between them. Had she and Zak gotten married? Mom would've known, but the only reason I stayed in touch was her promise never to mention his name. I was like an elephant. Not only would I never forget, I would never forgive any of them either.

CHAPTER TWO

Despite my assurances that I was fine, my parents worried about me because I was still alone and unmarried, a sin right up there with any of the Seven Deadly Ones as far as they were concerned. At thirty-two, I should have a husband and be pumping out grandchildren, not living on my own and working day and night—an exaggeration on her part, but at times, it was almost true. *Power and Light*, the name I'd given to the company I'd purchased from Jake Porter, was solidly in the black, but it had taken months of long hours and sweat equity to get there. Now and then, I did have people do a doubletake when I showed up to do their electrical work, but this was the twenty-first century and as I constantly reminded myself, I didn't need anyone or anything other than Frodo to be complete. I'd yet to convince Mom and Dad of that.

Was I lonely? Occasionally, but for the most part, work kept me busy, I had an entire library at my disposal for the downtime, and Frodo's purrs always made me feel better. I owned my home and my business, had the career I'd always wanted, and not only were all my bills paid, but I also had money in the bank. As my accountant put it, I was financially solvent. I'd even managed to lose ten kilos since moving here, even a bit from my boobs. What more could a girl want?

A lover, you say? No, thanks. I'd tried the romance, flowers, and happily ever after scenario, and it had blown up in my face. That wasn't to say I didn't date. I went out now and then and even made it to the sheets on occasion, but as I'd learned the hard way, sex had nothing to do with love. There was no way that I was going to get serious about anyone ever again. One massive heartbreak had left me hemorrhaging. I didn't need another.

I'd just finished getting into my work boots and coveralls and had replenished my toolbox when the phone rang. Reaching over, I grabbed the handset on the desk.

"*Power and Light*. Marissa speaking."

"Rissa, it's me. I've tried your cell a dozen times, and it keeps going to voice mail," she admonished. "I thought something was wrong. I've been worried sick."

"Sorry about that," I apologized, realizing that not being able to reach me had upset her, no doubt bringing back memories of the week it had taken before I'd called anyone five years ago. "I forgot it in the truck last night, and it's out of juice." I glanced at the device charging on the desk. "You don't normally call during the week. What's up?"

As a rule, Marley called on Sunday afternoons, the one day a week I had to myself.

She laughed. "An electrician who runs out of power—only you could do that. I was afraid ... I know what day this is, but I've been waiting for hours to give you my news. I hope it'll cheer you up."

I wasn't unhappy, but like my parents, Marley, or Kid as I called her, had trouble understanding my decision and choice. She worked at the Canadian Embassy in London, as executive assistant to the ambassador, the Right Honorable Jameson Bolt. She'd been there more than five years, thankfully having left Cedar Lake before my life had taken a nosedive, and while I missed her, she was living her dream. The five-hour time difference usually wasn't a problem, but there were occasions when Marley wanted to speak to me right away, and calls at four in the morning weren't always appreciated. Maybe the fact that I'd left the cell phone in the truck last night had been a good thing.

"Well, you have me now, but I have a job in half an hour. So, what's the big news? Mom and Dad are supposed to be in London this week, right?"

"No. Next week. They're in Iceland right now. Their cruise ship gets into Southampton on Monday, and they'll stay here with me for a week before going on to France. Rissa, I have the best news. Can you guess what it is?"

I rolled my eyes. Why did she do this? She'd call me with great news, and now I had to play *Twenty Questions* to get the information out of her! Some things never changed.

I checked my watch. I still had half an hour. Knowing she would expect me to at least give it the old college try, I sighed.

"Your contract got extended?" That would make her deliriously happy since her current assignment ended this year. She claimed she wasn't ready to return to Canada or get posted elsewhere.

"Not yet, but way better than that." Marley giggled.

"You're going to meet King Charles, up close and personal?"

She'd gushed about the few times she'd met the late Queen Elizabeth and other members of the royal family, like the Duke and Duchess of Sussex before they'd moved to Canada and later to the States, and the Duke and Duchess of Cambridge before they'd become the Prince and Princess of Wales. She'd attended functions where she'd hobnobbed with the rich and royal. Her boyfriend was the son of a Duke, although not the one in line for the title.

"Duh!" I imagined the eye roll. "I've already met him as well as Queen Camilla. I am the ambassador's executive assistant, after all, but I've also got friends in high places now. Come on. Try harder. Try something more personal."

While Marley had always loved guessing games, I never had—nor did I like surprises.

"I give up. Just tell me." I waited. "What? ... Marley, are you still there? Am I supposed to use the Force? Don't leave me hanging. What's your news?"

"Aaron asked me to marry him," she said, her voice filled with joy. "Rissa, I'm so happy, I'm afraid to pinch myself in case it's all a dream. He proposed last night. He took me to Renfield House for dinner, that's where the Duke and Duchess live in London, and popped the question after dessert. You should see my ring! It's a family heirloom that used to belong to his grandmother." She squealed with excitement. "As soon as I said yes, his parents were back with champagne to toast the occasion."

My jaw gaped, and I dropped into the chair. My sister was going to marry an aristocrat?

"Holy cow patties. Are you serious? You're going to be a lady, I mean as in Lady Broadmere?"

"I am, and I want you to be my Maid of Honor."

Tears brimmed my eyes. No wonder she was excited. She and Aaron Sykes, millionaire playboy, horse aficionado, and youngest son of the Duke of Habersham, had met when she'd first moved to London. She'd run into him, quite literally, when she'd been visiting the Tower of London on one of her days off. The man had knocked her off her feet while he'd spilled tea all over himself. She hadn't realized who he was, but there had been chemistry there, and after profuse apologies on both sides, she'd offered to get him another cup of tea. From there they'd moved on to dating. It wasn't until things got serious between them that he revealed his true identity and had taken her to meet the family. As expected, because if anyone was a people person, it was Marley, the family had loved her and had welcomed her. Now, it seemed they were ready to let her into their exalted ranks, too. My sister. A royal. Who would've guessed?

"Marley, that's wonderful news. Congratulations, and I'm honored to stand with you on your wedding day." I dismissed all the problems that taking an unexpected holiday at this time of year would mean for me, not to mention my abject fear of pomp, circumstance, and almost anything that would require me to dress up for the occasion. "Have you got a date in mind?"

"We do. How do you fancy a summer vacation in the English countryside? Aaron wants the wedding to take place at Knightsbridge, the family estate, and since Mom and Dad are here ... There will be extended family, quite a few with pedigrees actually, and some of Aaron's friends and business acquaintances. I'll limit myself to the people at the embassy and the Canadian ex-pats I've met since moving here. With Mom and Dad already in Europe, the timing's perfect. The estate is breathtaking. Come for a month so you can enjoy the place. If Mom and Dad insist, we can have a reception in Cedar Lake in the fall after we get back from our Australian honeymoon. Aaron spends a fair amount of time in Canada, so it won't be a problem. Did I tell you that he owns a ranch only an hour away from Cedar Lake?"

"No, you didn't mention that."

"He's into horses and started his own stud and stable. He has several horses with impressive pedigrees, and is looking to expand the reach and reputation of his stable."

"Is he thinking of moving to the colony?" I assumed a snobby British accent, or at least what I thought might pass for one.

She laughed. "You do have an ear for accents. We aren't planning to move to Canada. He has other business interests that will keep us in the UK, but we'll visit, of course. He loves it there and never misses a chance to attend the Calgary Stampede. I haven't been in years, but I'll be joining him in July. At any rate, the wedding will be a small one by peer standards, but that's all I want."

Small probably meant at least two hundred guests, half of them or more with titles, but I wouldn't miss my baby sister's wedding for the world. I would feel like a fish out of water, but if my ancestors could swim out of the primordial muck onto shore, the least I could do was get all gussied up for one day. Family was family, and you did everything you could for them.

"A vacation in the UK sounds awesome, but I can't be away from *Power and Light* for too long. I have a business to run. What exact date did you have in mind for the wedding?"

"I figured you'd say that. The date is set for Saturday, August fifteenth. If you can be here for the first, we can have a few days in London for dress fittings and to see things before heading to the country. Rissa, there's so much I want to show you."

"And so much I want to see," I answered, her excitement contagious and all but obliterating my envy.

As the eldest, I should've married first, but my ship had sailed five years ago today—sailed? Let me rephrase that. It had been blown out of the water, torpedoed, and sunk by Ken and Karen. Someday, I might get over the heartbreak enough to thank them for saving me from making the biggest mistake of my life. If my fiancé couldn't be faithful before the wedding, the odds weren't good that he would be after.

The shop door opened, admitting Bridget. She carried two extra-large coffee cups. I mouthed, "Thank you," and pointed at the phone, adding, "My sister."

"I can make arrangements to take ten days off," I continued, considering there was a four-day week in there. "Let me contact the airline and see what's available during the first week. I can email you after I know what's what—"

"Stop," Marley cried. "You don't have to make any arrangements. If you can fly out during the first week of August, I'll take care of it, or rather Aaron will. He insists on covering your travel as well as the cost of all four gowns and—"

"Four gowns!" The words exploded from my mouth, cutting her off as effectively as she'd done me. "Why in God's name do I need four dresses?"

"Not dresses, although you'll need at least six of those, but gowns for the formal evening occasions—the dinner where you'll be presented to my future-in-laws, the Duke and Duchess of Habersham, the rehearsal dinner, the wedding ceremony itself, and the wedding meal in the evening. They do things differently here, and the duke is a stickler for protocol. If His Majesty King Charles III is receiving, you'll need something special for that, too. Dinner each night is formal, but you can wear the same dress more than once, changing it up with different jewelry and stuff."

"Wait a minute. Are you saying King Charles might be at your wedding?" I wasn't quite ready to fraternize with royalty. Not only did I not know the etiquette, I wasn't even sure I would be able to get my mouth to work in such lofty company—either that or I'd put both feet in it and choke.

Marley chuckled. "I doubt that, but he and the duke are good friends, so he could decide to drop by unannounced, especially if he's in residence at Highgrove House. It's not far from Knightsbridge. He used to do so quite often before he ascended the throne, but don't worry about it. If he does come, I'll teach you to curtsy properly. It's not that hard."

"For you, maybe, but I'll probably fall flat on my face."

I pictured myself in some huge frilly dress with a bird-shaped fascinator on my head, flat on my face on a lawn so green that it looked fake, with the dress puffed up into the air and my thong on display. That wasn't the Canadian end of things I wanted the world to see.

She laughed. "You'll be fine. And don't worry about clothes. We'll get that all taken care of when you get here. Now, you go do what you have to do while I call Mom and Dad and give them the great news. Oh, and as soon as I can, I'll send you the information the dressmaker needs. Mom mentioned that you've lost weight."

"I have," I admitted, a touch of pride in my voice. "But as much as I'd like to chat a little longer, I have a major client sweltering in the heat with an air conditioner that isn't working. I'll do the measuring thing as soon as you send me the information, and email you the numbers. Give my best to Aaron and tell him I said he's the lucky one. I am very happy for you. Love you, Kid."

"Love you more."

The phone went dead.

"You look happy and here I expected to find you down in the dumps," Bridget came around and

handed me my coffee. "Double-double with sweetener."

I reached for the cup. "Thanks. Not going to mope today. I've just had the best news. Marley's getting married to a lord no less, and I'm going to be her Maid of Honor. Since my future brother-in-law is going to pay to get me there, you're going to get extra paid vacation this summer. In addition to the last weeks of July, you'll get the first two weeks of August. I'll get Jake to cover for me, and I'll see if Cathy Lewis is available to handle the phone and the store for the extra days. I'll be back here by the eighteenth to start that rewiring job at the school. It'll be business as usual for June and July. I'll have to do some shopping before I go. I don't want to look like I just dropped off the turnip truck. Rachel's bound to be able to fix me up. She's been dying to get me into *The Oasis,* her clothing store. So what do you think? Will that vacation time work for you?"

Bridget smiled. "It'll be perfect." Her cheeks reddened. "My mother called this morning," she added sheepishly.

My eyebrows disappeared under my bangs. "Your mother? I didn't realize you were on speaking terms with your parents. When did that happen?"

"I wasn't, not because I didn't try, but ... long story short, Dad had a health scare last month, and they've come to realize that life is too short to worry about what people will say. They want to reconcile and have asked Oli and me to come for a visit this summer. Those extra days are perfect." She swiped at her eyes. "I didn't realize how much I missed them until I heard her voice. I named my son after my father, even though he's never seen him."

I pulled her into my arms. "It's going to work out, you'll see." I stepped back, surprised by my show of affection. As a rule, I was one of the few people I knew who still maintained their COVID distance. "Now, if I don't get over to the Cooper house and fix their air conditioning, we may both need to look for new jobs." I stepped away and turned back, reaching for the boxed fan on the counter. "You've got my schedule if you need me. I penciled in a one o'clock job at the mayor's house. I'll see you Monday. Let the answering machine pick up any calls after three. I'll get to them when I get home."

I headed to the door.

"Wait," she cried. "Don't forget this." She handed me my charged cell phone.

I shook my head. "What would I do without you?"

Bridget smiled. "You'd manage. You always do."

* * *

It was after nine when I pulled my work van around back and dragged my tired ass out of it. All I wanted was to get out of these hot, smelly clothes and get to bed. I could probably use a drink, considering the day I'd had, but *Callaghan's*, the bar across the street, was busier than normal. On Saturdays, they offered a five-dollar specialty cocktail and Karaoke.

I'd gone over there once or twice, sitting with some of the regulars, but Saturdays drew a different crowd, and a woman alone at the bar often attracted the wrong company. Noah, the bartender, was a friend and always looked out for me, but tonight, I would prefer to wrestle alligators rather than be sociable. That yucky feeling from this morning was still there ... as if anything else could go wrong. I clung to my memory of Marley's excited voice, the only good thing to come from this lousy day.

Most days, things went smoothly. Not today. Things had gotten off to a rocky start when I discovered that the reason the Cooper air conditioner wasn't working was that mice had moved into it over the winter and chewed through a couple of cables. Did I mention that I hated rodents? I relocated the nest—thankfully the occupants weren't home at the time—replaced the cables, and got the unit working again, but that made me half an hour late for my next job, and it snowballed from there.

Skipping lunch to put up Regina Wendel's ceiling fan got me back on track for a bit, but I cut myself trying to get the damn box open. It wasn't a serious cut, but I'd added blood to the unknown substances on my overalls. From there, I headed over to the Jonson house to see what was wrong with their heat pump. By then, the temperature had risen over thirty-five degrees Celsius and that didn't include the humidex. Face covered by an industrial mask that made breathing difficult, I crawled through layers of fluffy pink insulation in their attic before replacing the wiring and getting the damn thing working again. Somewhere in that blown-in insulation, I'd lost my favorite screwdriver. Two hours later, skipping dinner to get the lights working at the Oakleys—she'd blown a breaker plugging in too many things on the same circuit— both batteries on my power drill died, leaving me to tighten the screws by hand, aggravating the damn cut that had started bleeding again. The next time I woke up feeling like I had today, I would pull the blankets over my head and stay in bed.

I grabbed my toolbox and cell phone from the back of the van, locked it, and then opened the shop's rear door, keying in the alarm code before the thing went off. I removed my work boots and slipped off my dirty overalls, revealing the faded blue tank top and Daisy Dukes I'd donned under them this morning. Yanking the elastic band out of my hair, I shook my head before finger-combing my tresses. While my blond hair was fine and straight, Marley had masses of gorgeous deep brown curls, another thing I envied about my sister, along with Mom's olive complexion. Like my father's mother, I could get sunburned sitting in the shade.

Marley getting married. I could hardly get my head around it. Mom and Dad must be thrilled. All the hoopla over this wedding would probably keep them off my back until Christmas, but then they would be at it again with a vengeance.

On the plus side, this was one wedding where it was unlikely that I would have to do the dance of shame, a custom that dated back to my mother's French Canadian roots where the elder unmarried sibling was forced to dance in a washtub as punishment for not getting married first. In some places, the washtub was replaced by big, ugly, work socks, but the results were the same. It was also a way to raise money for the newlyweds since people paid to dance with the humiliated older sibling, as well as a means of announcing that said person was available. Surely to God, the English peerage had moved beyond that point. Tradition might be important, but enough was enough.

If I got really lucky, it wouldn't be long before Marley and Aaron became parents. That would keep Mom and Dad busy, and if the newlyweds spent part of the time at Cedar Lake ... it would be all good. I yawned. It was time to stop dreaming and get on with things.

I plugged in the two dead batteries to recharge them and dumped my overalls into the basket with the other two pairs. I owned three sets, but the ones I'd worn today had been the cleanest of the bunch and now, they were filthy. It was probably time that I washed them, not that regular soap did much good on those set-in stains. Since next week promised to be just as busy as this one had been, I would do laundry tomorrow. For now, the gungy things could sit here with the others, along with the smelly work boots. After spraying the inside of them with deodorizer, I gave my feet a shot of spray and slipped on my sandals.

Going into the bathroom, I washed my hands thoroughly, disinfecting the cut that stung like hell. I dried it and put on a clean bandage and went into the office to check the phone messages. There was nothing that couldn't wait until Monday morning. Satisfied that I was finally done for the day, I made myself a note to pick up a new flat-nose screwdriver and another battery tomorrow, then set the alarm and left the shop by the front door since that exit was closer to the stairs leading to the apartment. There was a newer model sedan parked in front of the shop. Had it been there earlier? I couldn't remember.

The wind rustled the new leaves on the trees beside the building. The night air was slightly cooler than it had been earlier in the day, and I inhaled deeply. I longed for a shower, something to eat, and the peace and quiet of my air-conditioned apartment. Moving around to the side of the building to the covered staircase, I jumped when a man materialized before me.

"Hello, Marissa."

I yelped, almost wetting myself, completely forgetting all of the self-defense moves I'd perfected over the years. Since I had keyless electronic locks, I had nothing in my hands that I could use as a weapon.

"Ken." I would've recognized him anywhere. How could I not when he made regular appearances in my nightmares? "What the hell is wrong with you? You scared the living daylights out of me. If I had a heart condition, I'd be lying dead on the pavement at your feet. Better yet, if I had a gun or a knife, you would be dead." I glared at him, my face no doubt some vivid shade of puce. "What are you doing here?"

He chuckled and held up his hands in surrender. "You never fail to surprise me. I didn't mean to scare you, but it's nice to see you again. I'll admit I was hoping for a warmer reception, but I suppose it's the one I deserve, given the circumstances. I'm in town, and I thought I'd drop by." He shrugged.

I raised my eyebrows and took a good look at him. In the glow of the light from the streetlamp, I noted the casual pants he wore with a golf shirt, not the usual tattered jeans and t-shirt he'd opted for when he wasn't at work. Even his runners had been replaced by Oxfords. He'd packed on some muscle over the last five years—could he have cut back on the food and booze? As well, he'd changed the way he wore his light brown hair. Instead of the messy mop hairstyle, he now appeared polished with a side part that reminded me a little of Superman, especially with the curl falling forward over his brow. He was clean-shaven, having given up his scruffy beard. He might be more attractive than I recalled, but one thing about him hadn't changed. He was a bald-faced liar.

Nobody just dropped into Brockton. It was a small town off the beaten path. The was no major highway running through it. I still didn't understand how I'd managed to find it in the first place.

"I doubt that. So, what do you want?" I stood in what Bridget liked to call my Wonder Woman stance, daring him to keep lying to me.

He shook his head and smiled. "I'll say one thing. Your attitude may not have changed, but the rest of you has. You look fantastic. You always did have great legs, and now the rest of you..."

He eyed me up and down, his leer making me more than a little uncomfortable. I tugged at the bottom of my shorts.

I snorted. "Thanks, but seriously, Ken, what are you doing here?"

"I came specifically to see you," he said, his tone soft. "I've missed you, Marissa, we all have."

As if! To tease and humiliate maybe. To rub my face in the dirt of my degradation, probably, but miss me? Not in a million years. You had to like people to miss them, and if there was one thing I knew, neither Ken nor his sister Karen had ever liked me.

He shuffled his feet awkwardly, placing more weight on one than the other, bringing my attention back into focus. There was something in his eyes I didn't recognize. Could it be insecurity? Maybe even a bit of uncertainty? Was it possible that the self-proclaimed gift to women was nervous? With me? Impossible, and yet? For a moment, he didn't seem like the self-centered, self-assured man I thought I knew.

"I dropped by earlier and your secretary told me you'd be done around nine, so I checked into the motel down the road and came back a little while ago to wait for you. I'd like to sit down and talk. Have you eaten? The receptionist at the motel says that place has decent food." He pointed to *Callaghan's.*

The day from hell had just gotten worse. What could we possibly have to talk about, especially today of all days—or had my humiliation been of no consequence to him? Fate had tried to warn me, but...

"I'm pretty tired," I hedged, my stomach gurgling loudly enough to drown out the sound of a souped-up car racing down the street. What next? Would I fart and completely disgrace myself? I smirked and shrugged.

"You may be tired, but you're hungry, too. Come on. Can't we bury the hatchet for a while and just be two old friends sharing a meal and some company?"

Friends? Were we ever really friends? We'd certainly parted as enemies. Had I had a hatchet five years ago, his back wouldn't have been my first target, but it would've been a close second. My stomach gurgled again, determined not to be ignored.

"Fine. I am hungry. Let me go upstairs and change. Why don't I meet you over there in ten minutes?"

"Okay, but I don't see why you need to. You look sexy as hell in those short shorts and tousled hair." He held up his hand before I could comment. "I mean that as a compliment, so don't bite my head off. I'll get us a table and order drinks—you do drink, don't you or are you still vice free?"

"You mean, am I still the Ice Queen?" I used the name he'd given me in the past.

He winced. "Ouch, I guess I was a little hard on you back then. In my way, I did have a reason, but I've changed. Give me a chance to prove it."

My eyes opened wider. "Why the hell would you want to prove anything to me?"

CHAPTER THREE

Ken rubbed the nape of his neck and shuffled his feet once more.

I blinked. This was new. Ken Atkinson was uncomfortable. I should be enjoying his distress, but I wasn't. I felt sorry for him ... maybe because I'd been there myself more often than I could count.

"Life is full of opportunities," he began, shifting from one foot to the other. "Most of the time, they go by unnoticed. A close encounter with an elk about six months after you left Cedar Lake reminded me that life can be cut short and gave me time to take a good look at myself. I didn't like what I saw. When I got back on my feet as it were, I made a few changes—for the better, I hope. I've tried to clean up my act and make amends. Will you give me a chance to apologize to you?"

Near-death experiences could change people, even those as morally corrupt as Ken. I nodded.

"Why not. The people here gave me a second chance." Wasn't paying it forward a thing? They'd helped me; I would help him. "Noah will have a drink special tonight. Just get me one of those and a bacon cheeseburger and fries." Normally, I avoided carb-loaded dishes like that but I needed comfort food tonight. I would jog an extra half-mile tomorrow.

He frowned. "Noah? Your Aunt Yvette didn't mention that you were seeing someone."

Was he jealous? Good grief. He'd changed all right—he'd lost his mind.

"It's a small town, and I'm the only electrician. Even if I were seeing someone, I doubt Ma Tante Yvette would know about it." A light went on inside my head. "Was she the one who told you where I was?" I'd begged Mom and Dad not to tell anyone.

"Yeah. I was at the bank getting things organized and mentioned that I was traveling this way. She suggested I look you up."

I nodded. Obviously, members of the family didn't fit into Mom's definition of *anyone*, and Yvette was her sister and my godmother ... not the fairy tale kind, but she probably thought she was doing me a favor. I unlocked the door to the stairs.

"I won't be long." I closed the door before he tried to follow me in and rushed up the stairs.

I hurried to the bathroom, answered Mother Nature's call, and then changed since these shorts left me cheekier than usual. I washed my hands and face, replaced the bandage once more, and then reached for the hairbrush to tame my mane, pulling it into a messy bun. I added moisturizer and lip gloss, the usual extent of my makeup routine.

I put on clean underwear, the jeans I'd picked up last fall, and a newer, sleeveless, black silk blouse that still fit decently. I might have no reason to want to impress the man, but I was proud enough to give it my best shot. After all, I would know people in the bar, and who didn't want to go the extra mile now and then? I added my favorite gold hoops to my earlobes, spritzed the air with *La Vie Est Belle,* the perfume Marley had given me for my birthday, and walked through it. Then, I grabbed my small purse, shoving my wallet and cell phone inside it, before stuffing my feet into my sandals once more.

I was crossing the kitchen when Frodo loudly informed me that I'd missed providing him with dinner. Quickly opening a can of tuna, my way of apologizing, I filled his water dish and left while he was gorging himself. I went down the stairs, surprised to find Ken still waiting for me.

"I thought you were going to go over and order."

His gaze raked me, his mouth splitting into a grin.

"I wasn't sure you were coming back, not that I would blame you if you did stand me up. Now, I get to walk in with the prettiest girl in town. You look fantastic."

I rolled my eyes, secretly pleased that he'd been forced to admit that, but unwilling to take anything he said at face value.

"You haven't seen the girls in this town. But since I look enough like your sister to be mistaken for your twin and hers, there's something creepy about the way you're looking at me." The heat in his green eyes was more than a little unnerving.

Ken burst out laughing. "How did I ever miss your unique sense of humor? You may look like her. but honey, you aren't my sister, and never were. We're simply kissing cousins. Maybe it's time we started acting like them instead of sparring partners." He chuckled. "Don't worry, I'm not going to kiss you right now."

"Good, because I've been known to bite the hand that feeds me."

He reached for my arm and tucked it into his. "I'll remember that, but the images it conjures up are intriguing, but for now let's go and get something to eat. You were always cranky on an empty stomach."

Too stunned to do anything but gawk, I allowed him to lead me across the street.

As I'd expected, *Callaghan's* was crowded with a mix of both regulars and strangers who made their way here each weekend for the drinks and the chance to be singing stars. While most were mediocre at best, there was always a winner or two amongst the regulars. I removed my arm from Ken's and pointed to the far corner away from the stage. There were a couple of empty tables since most people preferred sitting closer to the performers and the dance floor. I wasn't planning on doing any singing or dancing tonight. I might belt out a tune or two in the shower or the van, but I didn't perform in front of an audience.

Lydia Montrose, a Karaoke regular and the lead singer in the church choir, was belting out Tina Turner's "What's Love Got to Do With It?" a rather prophetic choice for the occasion.

We'd just settled at the table when Ginny came over to take our order.

"Hey, Marissa. You don't usually come in on Saturdays." She eyed Ken as if he were a T-bone steak, and she hadn't eaten in days. "I didn't know you had a brother!"

Rolling my eyes at the way she was exposing her substantial cleavage, I shook my head.

"I don't. Ken, Ginny. He and I are distant cousins and grew up together out west. He's just passing through and decided to look me up. What's tonight's drink special?"

She ignored my question and focused on Ken. "Well, if you decide to stick around, I'll be happy to show you the town while Marissa's working."

Ken surprised me. Instead of taking her up on her obvious offer, he shook his head. "Thanks, but I'll be leaving tomorrow, and I'm sure Marissa can show me whatever there is to see."

Put in her place—even Ginny recognized a brush-off when she heard one—she nodded.

"What can I get you to drink?"

"I'll have a large draft—what's on tap?"

She rattled off the night's beer selection.

"Make it a Beau's, and Marissa will have the drink special. As well, can you bring two bacon cheeseburgers and fries?" He smiled at her and soothed her ruffled feathers.

"Thanks, Ginny," I said, reminding her that I was still there.

The Tina Turner wannabe was replaced by the Smiths singing "Islands in the Stream."

"This is a nice place," Ken said, looking around. "It reminds me of *The Vault*."

The Vault was a bar and grill located inside what had once been a bank back home. Zak had taken me there a few times. I'd found it noisy, so we'd avoided it, preferring some of the smaller, quieter places, but I didn't want to think about Zak, especially not tonight. That weird feeling persisted even though Ken's arrival had been unexpected. Surely there couldn't be another shoe waiting to drop?

"Other than wanting to talk to me and apologize for being a jerk most of our lives, why are you here?"

At that moment, Ginny returned with the drinks, preventing Ken from answering my question. She set the large draft in front of him and the cocktail coupe filled with something pretty and very pink, garnished with a basil leaf, in front of me. I sipped, pleasantly surprised by the tangy strawberry taste.

"This is good." I licked my lips. "What's it called?"

"It's a Match." She shook her head. "Weird name, I know, but somehow it fits."

I chuckled and sipped again. "What's in it?"

"Lemon vodka, strawberries, basil, a jalapeño disk, lemon juice, and simple syrup. Noah puts it all through the blender and strains it. The drinks are selling well." She grinned at Ken. "Food won't be long."

Turning on her heels, she hurried over to serve a table full of guys who'd just come in.

Ken raised his mug to me. "Here's to getting reacquainted and second chances."

I clinked my glass against his. Second chances? At what? Did I want to get reacquainted? Probably not, but I was hungry and tired, and this drink was delicious. I took another sip and set the glass down on the table.

"Now, why are you here? Brockton's a long way from the Alberta oil fields and Cedar Lake. Nobody shows up unintentionally." Apparently, according to Jake Porter, I'd been Divine Intervention—not that I believed in that—but even if I did, I couldn't imagine why the Lord would send Ken here.

He put down his beer mug. "I told you. I came to see you and that's God's truth, but I'm also on my way to Montreal. I fly to London tomorrow night. I changed jobs after the accident and dedicated myself to looking after the planet rather than adding to its problems. I'm now working with a team of researchers committed to green energy. I'll be spending six months in Newcastle. We're looking at ways to make traditional energy sources greener. While I'm there, I'll spend some time with

Karen. She and a couple of her friends moved there just before the pandemic. She loves it."

Other than not thinking about Zak, I also didn't want to think about Karen. Just hearing her name soured my stomach.

"My sister Marley's still in England," I said, pulling the conversation away from his sister.

"That's right. She moved there about five years ago, just a few months before you left town. I recall my mother saying yours had been devastated to lose both her girls so close together."

I certainly didn't want to dwell on that!

"Mom didn't lose us. We didn't die or get abducted by aliens. We simply moved to get on with our lives, and speaking of lives, Marley called this morning to announce that she's getting married in August. I'll be going over there to be in the wedding party." I took another sip. The drink was going down smoothly, and I was beginning to relax. Maybe this impromptu meeting wouldn't be so bad after all.

"In London?" he asked, his face creasing into a smile. "I could probably get some time off and come to see you. I could even be your plus one."

I shook my head. Ken? My plus one? Never going to happen.

"Unfortunately, no. The wedding's taking place at Knightsbridge, her fiancé's family estate. Can you believe it? She's marrying a lord. She'll be Lady Broadmere." The drink beckoned once more, and I sipped. "As for a plus one, I don't know if that's even a thing over there. The place will teem with lords, dukes, earls, and whatever other titles they have in the family. Marley's future father-in-law is friends with the king, for heaven's sake. Can you see it? Me meeting the king? I'll be as awkward and out of place as the proverbial country mouse visiting the city."

He shook his head. "I have no doubt you'll rise to the occasion. You always do, and you'll look smashing as the Brits say. But I'm serious. If you need a date over there, I'm your man."

The earnest expression on his face threw me. I couldn't recall any time in the thirty-two years that we'd been alive when Ken had offered to do something nice for me without an agenda.

"I'll know more after I talk to her, but if I have time to do any traveling around while I'm there, I'll let you know. It might be nice to see a friendly face." Not that I would've considered his to be one an hour ago.

Ginny set the two platters of food in front of us. "Do you want another?" She indicated the empty cocktail glass.

When had I finished it?

Ken emptied his mug. "Bring us both refills and some water." He smiled at me. "I recall how you always had to have water with your meals."

Ginny cocked her head, her eyes filling with a *so that's how it is,* look. As much as I wanted to set the record straight, I couldn't figure out how to do it without coming off bitchy, and truth be told, it was kind of flattering to know he'd recalled something like that about me.

"So tell me, Marissa, do you miss home?" Ken squirted ketchup onto his fries.

"At times, but I don't miss the vicious cold and the snow in winter," I answered, going on to discuss life in small-town Ontario, not that it was much different from life in small-town Alberta. Everybody knew everybody else's business, and gossip was one of life's little pleasures.

I bit into my burger. As always, the food was delicious, and I was ravenous. I reached for the water to wash down the burger. Who would've believed Ken had noticed my little quirk?

While we ate, he brought me up to speed on the comings and goings of the people I'd known all my life—who'd died, who'd married, who'd divorced, who'd had a baby, as well as who'd moved away. Some of his stories were funny while others brought with them a touch of nostalgia. Life had gone on without me, and that was good, wasn't it? The one person he didn't mention was Zak, and I didn't ask. Mom had tried to bring up his name, but when I'd threatened to go incommunicado again, she'd stopped. What Zak did was his business and none of mine.

"What about you? I saw that you owned *Power and Light*. As the only electrician in town, you must be doing well. It was your dream to own your own business, wasn't it?"

I finished my second drink and followed it with a half-glass of water. Ginny appeared with another I didn't recall ordering, but hey, I was having fun for the first time in forever.

"It was one of them," I admitted, not dwelling on the bucket list items I'd crossed off, not because I'd completed them but because they would never be fulfilled. "I've come to know a lot of people, and I'm happy here. Mom and Dad would like to see me come back to Cedar Lake, but Marley and Aaron will be there long before I will. You may have heard that a British lord is starting a horse breeding ranch about an hour out of town."

He nodded. "The old Appleton farm. Yeah. I haven't been out there, but they did a lot of rebuilding last year, and I heard that the place has impressive breeding stock. He's got a Black Arabian worth a fortune. Super-fertile stallions like that can ejaculate daily, producing over twenty million dollars' worth of semen during the eight-month stud season. The high-quality semen is frozen in straws for sale. So that's him, your future brother-in-law?"

"Yeah. Aaron Sykes, Lord Broadmere, and that was more information about stallions than I needed." I laughed and went on to talk about Bridget and how helpful Regina had been when I'd bought the business from Jake and how he still supported me. "I'll be taking on a co-op student from the high school in the fall. Georgia sees me as an inspiration." I shrugged. "I'll bet you never expected that."

"I never expected you to leave Cedar Lake," he said softly.

Swallowing another mouthful of the pink concoction, I tried to ignore the intense gleam in his eyes and started telling him about some of the more interesting things that had happened such as coming across a wasps nest in a power box or dealing with mice in an attic. "The worst thing that ever happened to me was getting called out in the middle of the night after a storm to reconnect downed lines and encountering a skunk between me and the job. I must've bought every can of tomato juice in town to try and wash the stench off me. But I learned my lesson. I don't go anywhere without a strong LED flashlight now and bear spray. It'll work on anything."

Ginny came and took away the dishes and replaced our drinks once more. I probably should've ordered coffee, but I wanted to sleep tonight and, truth be told, I was enjoying Ken's company, and that weird feeling was finally gone.

When Noah got up to sing Percey Sledge's "When a Man Loves a Woman," couples paired off on the dance floor, and it seemed quite natural to join them.

Ken held me close, and I relaxed against him, comfortable in his company despite our checkered past. He moved a little sluggishly, but as I recalled he'd never really liked dancing—at least not with me. The woodsy cologne he wore was familiar, reminding me of good times, and I settled against him, surprised by how well we fit together.

"Do you realize that it's been almost twenty years since we've danced together?"

I smirked. "I'd forgotten all about that." It had been at the eighth-grade graduation dance. "As I recall, your mother forced you to—"

"And you stepped on my toes." He chuckled, the sound rumbling in his chest under my cheek. "I came across the picture she took when I was going through some old photo albums. There were a lot of you, especially in those early birthday party photos."

"Yeah. Having one party instead of three somehow made sense to them back then." But I'd always felt as if I was missing out on having a birthday all to me. When Mom had decided I'd grown too old for parties, I'd missed those too, although Ken and Karen had partied on long after me. "Sorry about stepping on your toes. I wasn't much of a dancer."

He tightened his hold on me. "Well, you've certainly improved not that there was anything wrong with you back then."

"Did you forget your sister referring to me as a prancing baby elephant?"

He lowered his chin to rest it against my head. He chuckled, his chest rumbling beneath my ears. "Karen was a bitch. That girl was just jealous of you."

"Jealous of me? What was there to be jealous of?"

Ken didn't answer. The song ended, but we stayed on the floor as Noah moved into "My Special Prayer."

When the music stopped, we returned to the table and our drinks until the Smiths got up once more and sang another Kenny and Dolly duet. This time, it was "Love Lifted Me," and we joined the other couples again. Ken was might only have been a so-so dancer, but there was something comforting about being in the arms of an attractive man once more. Nothing could come of this impromptu reunion, but perhaps I was beginning to heal.

It was after midnight when I refused a fifth or was it a sixth cocktail?

"No, thanks. I've reached my limit, and I've got a big day tomorrow."

"Just bring the bill," he told Ginny before turning back to me.

"Working?" He pulled a credit card out of his wallet.

"I can pay for my own," I offered.

"Next time," he answered as if he expected there would be one. Maybe there would be while I was in the UK. "So are you working tomorrow?"

"Not as an electrician," I sighed. "It's paperwork and laundry with a little housework tossed in. If I get an emergency call, I'll take it, of course, but I usually use Sundays to catch up on the minutia of life. Normally, I would call home, but Mom and Dad are in Europe, so we're keeping in touch through Messenger when she has the Internet. When are you leaving for Montreal?"

"Unfortunately, by eight. It's a two-and-a-half-hour drive from here, and I have to meet my colleagues at eleven."

Should I offer to make him coffee and breakfast before he left? Probably not. I didn't want to send out any false messages, and given how late it was, how far behind I was in my sleep, not to mention how many cocktails I'd had, I would be lucky to crawl out of bed before noon.

Ginny brought over the bill. Ken paid it and, judging by the size of her eyes, added a generous tip. She grinned. "Come back again."

"I hope to," he answered.

Rather than say anything contradictory, I just nodded.

We stood and walked out of the bar, Ken taking my hand in his as we headed across the street. It never occurred to me to object. I was pleasantly relaxed, and he'd been the perfect companion all evening. I'd enjoyed reminiscing about the old days, surprised to find that it hadn't been all bad.

At the bottom of the stairs, he stopped and reached for my other hand.

"I enjoyed myself tonight, Marissa. It makes me regret even more the fact that I was such a jerk back then. When I was going through those old albums ... let me just say that I'm sorry. I know it can't undo all those years of bad behavior on my part but ... I liked you, you know, I liked you a lot— I still do, only now I'm brave enough to admit it. You know what a bitch my sister was, and you weren't the only one she picked on, although I'll admit I warranted a lot of it. You didn't. I didn't want Karen and her friends to tease me about the way I felt about you, so I played the bully until I came to believe my own crap. When you and Zak ... I called you the Ice Queen not because I thought you cold and unfeeling, but because I couldn't seem to thaw your heart when it came to me, not that I deserved it. If I'd stopped being an ass, you might've looked at me the way you looked at him.

And that's the other reason why I came to see you tonight."

His face was solemn, his eyes so sorrow-filled that I was afraid to hear what he had to say. Had something terrible happened to Zak? Was that why he'd never mentioned him until now? I might want to hate the man for betraying me the way he had, but I still loved him. Love and hate were sides of the same coin, but I'd been unable to flip it.

I wasn't prepared for even half of what Ken had said. If this confession went on much longer, we would attract the attention of the others leaving the bar. Should I invite him inside, or would that send the wrong message? Better to tough it out here.

"Given how serious you've become, I'm almost afraid to ask. What other reason do you have for being here?"

He released my hands. "This." He pulled a small brown envelope out of his pocket. "I won't be returning to Cedar Lake when my collaboration in the UK is over. I'll be working for the National Energy Board in Ottawa. That's only a little over an hour away. I'm hoping you'll be open to seeing me again. If tonight is anything to judge by, we get along well as adults. It's too bad it took Karen and me so long to grow up."

He continued before I could comment.

"Since Karen settled in England, Mom and Dad put the house up for sale. While they were cleaning and reconditioning the hot tub, they found it. At first, I thought it was Karen's, but then I realized it was yours."

He reached for my hand and poured out the contents of the envelope into my palm. I stared down at my platinum engagement ring as if it were a poisonous spider or some other venomous insect. The marquise diamond gleamed in the muted light, almost as if it were winking at me.

"Somehow, it ended up trapped under the skimmer. I would've expected it to be damaged, but I had Roy at *Spears Jewelers* clean it. If it had been gold or silver, it might not have survived, but platinum is a tougher metal."

That was why we'd chosen it. If I did get zapped at work and assuming I survived, the ring was unlikely to melt into me, having a much higher melting point than gold.

"I don't want this," I started, but he closed my fist over the ring before I could return it. "It belongs to Zak."

He shook his head. "I tried to give it to him, but he insisted that it's yours." He looked down at his shoes before looking back at me, his brow furrowed, his mouth a straight line, and his eyes filled with shame. "I'm not proud of this, but I have to be honest with you. I don't remember a lot about the night you left Cedar Lake, but knowing the way I used to behave when I over-indulged in liquor, I'm pretty sure I must've been a real ass. I stick to beer now and a lot less of it. We'd been drinking all day, and I was pissed at Molly Jones. She'd just dumped me for Carl Granger, and in my misery, I was hitting the bottle even harder than I normally did. Most of the guys were picked up around ten or so, but Zak had agreed to stick around and help me clean up, not that we were capable of doing anything by then. Karen finished work early. She wasn't feeling well—a headache or something, I don't know. I do recall her rant about not cleaning up our mess. At that point, Zak and I were almost comatose on the couch, watching the game. I recall asking her to make us another drink, and as God is my witness, after that, everything is blank."

I cocked my head to the left and backed away from him. The warm fuzzy feelings brought on by the cocktails vanished. The most hurtful and embarrassing moment of my life, one in which he'd featured predominantly, and he recalled none of it? How convenient for him. I squeezed my hand, the despised ring cutting into my palm. For the first time, I wondered what Zak had recalled, but being drunk was no excuse for what he'd done ... and Karen would've been stone-cold sober.

CHAPTER FOUR

Ken leaned against the door, seeming to understand my need for putting distance between us.

"When I got up in the morning with the headache from hell, Karen had gone to work, and Zak was on the couch. We were both confused because you were supposed to pick him up. He'd been trying to reach you on your cell phone, but every call went to voice mail. He called your parents' house and then his apartment. When he couldn't get you anywhere, he was like a man possessed, terrified that something horrible had happened."

I harrumphed. "I'll bet." It had. I'd seen his lady friend chowing down on him.

"Since he insisted, I called Karen at work to see if you'd been brought into the hospital, but she calmly explained that you'd come over to pick Zak up and that you and he had had a huge fight. For a second, we wondered if one of the guys had slipped something into our drinks, but none of them would've done something like that. That's when Karen told him you'd called off the engagement and had thrown your ring at him."

"That's what she said? That he and I had fought?"

"Yeah. Zak was stunned. Like me, he had no memory of you being there, nor could he understand why you'd fight, especially one that would cause you to break your engagement. Isn't that how you remember it?"

I shook my head. "Not exactly, but go on."

Ken frowned. "He was sure she was exaggerating, but while we searched for the ring all over the house, we never considered that it could be in the hot tub. Karen hadn't mentioned that. The fact that we couldn't find it upset him."

I was sure it had. He'd spent a fortune on what he'd called the perfect ring. So why hadn't he kept it when Ken had offered it to him? And why had Karen lied about what had happened? She knew exactly why I'd broken our engagement. What game had she been playing?

"When your parents got back, and he found out you'd left town," Ken continued, looking like someone allocuting at his trial, "Zak went crazy. Did your parents tell you that they'd been forced to call the police to get him to leave the house?"

My jaw dropped. "No, they never said a thing." Of course, I'd promised to stop calling if they mentioned his name, so that might've had something to do with it.

He reached over to touch my arm. "Eventually, because Zak's the best vet in the area, things settled down between them, but whenever he asked about you, all your mother would say was that you were alive and happy. The only reason your aunt gave me your address was my promise not to give it to him. Zak may still be my friend, but my word is my bond. I don't know what happened that night, what you two fought about, but I deeply regret any role I may have had in it."

A tear trickled down my cheek.

He brushed it away with the pad of his thumb. "I'm sorry. If I could undo whatever happened that night, I would."

Should I tell him the truth? Should I revisit the humiliation I'd felt seeing his sister giving my fiancé a blow job?

Karen knew exactly what had happened, but for her own reasons, had chosen to lie about it, and in doing so, had spared me being the butt-end of countless jokes. Why should I rip off that bandage again and lay it all out there? Why should I repeat his hateful words?

Ken had apologized. He might not know what he'd said, but he regretted whatever role he'd played in that mess. Was I a big enough person to forgive and forget? If I didn't, I would never be able to move on. My quarrel wasn't with him. It was with Zak and Karen.

"While my memories differ slightly from yours and Karen's, it's all water under the bridge now. None of it matters. Sometimes, what we think is a perfect relationship isn't. Zak and I were friends before we became lovers. We should've left it at that. You weren't responsible for the breakup. That was all on me. You live and learn. Now, I'm not sure what I'll do with this," I indicated the ring, "but thank you for tonight. I had a good time." But I wanted to be alone to lick my gaping wounds just as I'd done five years ago.

"Here." He handed me a business card. "If you call that number when you get to England, I'll get the message. Feel free to email me. I put my info on the back of the card. I understand if you need time, but I hope you'll call." He looked down at his feet once more. "Zak's still in love with you, Marissa. Maybe you need to give him a second chance ... at least explain what went wrong and clear the air between you."

"There's no air to clear. As far as I'm concerned, what we had was in the past. I've moved on. So should he," I lied. I was surprised that he and Karen hadn't done so together, but if she was in England and he was in Cedar Lake...

"That's all I wanted to know." He moved quickly, pulling me into his arms. "I said I wouldn't kiss you earlier, but..."

His mouth fastened on mine. Instinctively, my bruised soul responded, and I returned the kiss. When his tongue licked at my lips, I opened to him, enjoying the sensations I hadn't allowed myself to feel in years. I might've dated, even had sex, but I'd never let another man kiss me. As Julia Roberts said in *Pretty Woman*, kissing was too personal.

He slowly pulled his mouth away. "Damn, I wish I didn't have to leave tomorrow. Promise you'll call me when you get to England?"

I nodded. "I will ... and thanks again for tonight."

He looked into my eyes, searching for something...

"I could stay..."

I shook my head. "I don't think that would be a good idea. I'll call you when I get to England—I promise."

He shrugged, nodded, and walked over to the sedan I'd noticed earlier. Turning away, I unlocked the door and climbed the stairs once more. I carried the ring into my bedroom, opened my jewelry box, and dropped it inside. After completing my nightly ablutions, I crawled into bed and let the tears fall. Frodo, sensing my misery, jumped up on the bed and curled into me.

Nine Weeks Later

Why was it that when you had nothing of any significance to do, time crawled as if carried on the back of snails and slugs, but when you had something momentous on the horizon, it flew by faster than a supersonic jet at an air show?

June started with a return to normal weather patterns and business moved at the same speed it usually did. One day, I would be twiddling my thumbs between calls, wondering if I would make enough to pay the mortgage for the month, the next I would be running around like a chicken with my head cut off trying to stretch my eight-hour day to get everything done on time. The nights were the worst since I spent them tossing and turning, alternating between nightmares of what had happened five years ago and worrying about all the things that could and probably would go wrong when I finally made it to England. How on earth would I fit in with high society? Marley and I might just as well have been born on different planets. We were sisters, but we were as different as two people could possibly be. As Dad had always said, I'd been born full of piss and vinegar, doing things my own way, even when listening to others would've made things easier, and she'd been born full of sugar and honey, always the diplomat soothing the savage beasts around her to earn the life she wanted for herself.

The next thing I knew, it was July, and I didn't have enough time left to panic. There were jobs to finish, plans to make for after my return, the unenviable task of buying what Rachel and Bridget called appropriate clothes, and finally packing for my ten-day-sojourn in the UK. I couldn't call it a vacation because, from the timetable Marley had sent, I would scarcely have time to sleep, let alone relax until the wedding was over. By then, I would be too tired to do anything. Now that I'd completed all the jobs I'd scheduled and had assured myself that my livelihood would survive my three-week absence, I could finally worry about what came next.

I dropped Frodo off at the cat spa where he would be pampered and cared for until my return, a twelve-day cat vacation that cost more than twice my monthly mortgage, and then took the train to Dorval worrying not only about my pet but about my future. After a quick taxi ride to the airport, not feeling in the least bit confident, I checked in, got my boarding pass, went through security, and settled into the Maple Leaf Lounge, convinced that somewhere along the line I'd forgotten something. I noshed on veggies, cheese, and cold cuts, and sipped a beer as I waited for my call to board.

While I had Ken's card in my purse, I'd decided not to contact him before getting to England. It was true our time together had been enjoyable, as had his surprising goodnight kiss, but the more I thought about it, the more I realized that the evening five years ago hung between us like some damn Sword of Damocles, a sense of impending doom that I would do well to avoid. There was no way that I could enter into a relationship without coming clean about everything.

But was I ready to relive that humiliation? And while he might've called his twin a bitch, she was still his sister. If she hadn't revealed her role in all of this, did I have the right to do so? Would he even believe me or would he think I was making it all up, the way he and so many others had thought back in school when I've vented my displeasure? I'd lost countless hours of sleep and suffered through scores of nightmares imagining the pitfalls of it all.

With Rachel's help, I'd managed to get measured according to the particulars from Marley's dressmaker, and my sister had kept me in the loop concerning the wedding plans and the gowns being made specifically for me. I was amazed by the fact that all of the colors had been chosen with my fair skin in mind, and there wasn't a pastel in the lot. Nothing would make me look washed out and sickly. I wasn't much of a clothes horse, but the thought of those gowns was enough to bring out the giddy girl, the hidden Disney princess, in any woman, including a tomboy like me. I was anxious to try them on, an activity I usually hated. Knowing Marley's love for shopping, I was sure I would be donning and doffing dresses, hats, and shoes long after the novelty wore off.

From what I could see in the events' itinerary she'd sent me, I would spend more time changing clothes than I would spend attending the particular events scheduled, among which were a polo match, a few dinners, and other activities involving family and friends, and a trip to the opera. Multiple scenes from *Pretty Woman* came to mind. I would avoid ordering the "slippery little suckers," as Julia Roberts had called the escargots, not that I was particularly fond of snails. I might be the country mouse, but I sure as hell wouldn't look like one, and I needed to remember not to behave like one, too.

Mom was excited about her wardrobe and Dad's suits and tuxedos. The way she was carrying on, you would think she'd spent her entire life wearing sackcloth and ashes instead of some of the most fashionable outfits at the school where she'd taught for more than thirty-seven years. In Dad's case, a working cattle farmer, he'd probably never owned more than one suit at a time.

My mother had gone on and on about how I was to behave, almost as if she expected me to show up for breakfast in my coveralls and work boots, a stick of hay clenched in my teeth. Okay, so given the choice, I would be in jeans, running shoes, and a sweatshirt, but at least they would be clean.

Who in hell needed to change three or four times a day? Didn't they realize how much work that created for someone else? I had better things to do than dress for morning, afternoon, and then evening.

Still, not wanting to embarrass myself or anyone else, I'd bought a book on how to behave in formal situations and had memorized the table settings. I was still struggling with the need for three forks, three knives, and three spoons. Would the world come to an end if I ate my salad with the fish fork or cut my meat with the salad knife? And why did I need a demitasse spoon? And then there were all the ones above the plate as well as the glassware. Only people who didn't have to wash the dishes themselves did all of that, but as Mom kept saying, this was for Marley.

I'd logged onto a site that had taught me how to curtsy should the need arise. It had taken a fair amount of practice, especially in heels, but while I wasn't perfect, I didn't expect to fall flat on my face either. If an eight-year-old could do it, so could I.

Finally, I'd picked up a book on British royalty, etiquette, and how to address Royals should the need arise. King Charles and Queen Camilla were *majesties*, the Prince and Princess of Wales were *highnesses*, and the Duke and Duchess of Habersham, or any other duke and duchess for that matter, were *graces*. From there I was looking at *my lord* or *my lady*, *sir* or *ma'am*. Simple enough when meeting people in a one-on-one situation.

Everything was going well until I started to wonder about those awkward moments at the wedding functions where I was likely to run across a bunch of unknown ones all at the same time. What did you call a group of royals? Kings, queens, princes, and princesses could be called the Monarchy, but what about all the rest? Were they a choir, like angels, a bevy, like beautiful women, or a rafter, like turkeys? There were twenty different words to describe a group of geese ranging from a flock to a chevron, surely there was one for a gang of titled people. There was nothing in the book on it.

The garbled voice over the intercom announced my flight, and I made my way through the busy airport to the appropriate gate. While I wasn't much of a traveler, there was no doubt in my mind that Business Class was the way to go—not that I would be able to afford to travel this way on my own. This ticket cost more than I made in three months.

My fear that I would have to spend hours glued to a stranger evaporated when I was escorted to a pod seat beside a window. I stashed my carry-on bag overhead and settled into an amazingly comfortable seat with everything I could imagine at my fingertips. By some miracle, the seat beside me remained empty. Don't get me wrong. I'm not a snob. I can be a sociable as the next person, but I would prefer to do it on my own time and in my own circumstances. Having to be nice to a stranger for seven or eight hours didn't make my list. I mean what if I fell asleep and snored or drooled or God forbid farted? Things happened when you were asleep that you couldn't control. I was all about control.

After the Business Class passengers and people with disabilities or small children were seated throughout the Airbus, the remaining passengers boarded.

It seemed like no time before I was watching the scenery outside the window as the plane raced along the runway. We'd scarcely left the ground before the action started. I was offered a scented hot towel to clean my hands. Next, the flight attendant presented me with a small toiletry kit and offered me a drink.

I chose a champagne cocktail. After all, this was a cause for celebration. A short time later, she brought me a selection of cheese and crackers as well as the dinner menu.

I opted for the chicken dish. It came with a small salad, bread, oil for dipping, rice, seasonal mixed vegetables, and a luscious chocolate cake for dessert. Over the course of the meal, I had two glasses of white wine. I skipped the liqueur but indulged in the delicious truffles that followed. The last thing I wanted was to wake up with a splitting headache the way I had the morning after Ken's visit. Some activities were not to be repeated and drinking seven cocktails as Ginny had informed me I'd done, was one of them.

By now, it was after ten on my watch. The attendant came around with pillows and blankets and showed me how to fold my seat flat, providing me with a bed. The lights in the flight cabin dimmed. I put on the noise-canceling headphones provided and the sleep mask and closed my eyes. Despite the thoughts whirling inside my head, I slept for a few hours. It might not have been deep sleep, but it had been restful.

The lights in the cabin came on once again. Standing, I made my way to the bathroom. My polyester pantsuit and the yellow matching top hadn't wrinkled even though I'd slept in them, and I still looked presentable as Mom would say.

When I got back to my seat, the attendant had turned it into a chair once more and offered me coffee followed by a delectable hot breakfast. I raised the shade on the window please to see the sunrise. I glanced at my watch quickly and frowned. According to it, it wasn't yet two a.m. I'd left Montreal at nine p.m., which would've been two in the morning in London. The flight was almost seven hours long and we were expected to land at just after nine a.m. London time. No doubt jetlag would kick in at some point, but right now I was happy and excited to almost have reached my destination.

The *fasten your seatbelt* light came on, and within minutes the Air Canada plane touched down at Heathrow Airport, the second busiest International airport after Dubai, according to the article I'd read on the flight.

I looked out the window at the active airport as the plane taxied to its gate. The sun I'd watched rise was still shining, which had to be a good omen. Aaron was in Brussels until tomorrow evening when he, Mom, and Dad would return to London. Marley and I would spend the day at the dressmakers for final fittings. There were two events in London— the opera on Friday evening and a costume ball on Saturday. Why anyone would want to have a costume party so far away from Halloween was a mystery, but Marley had been gushing about how great the masquerade ball would be. Hopefully, the costume she was providing would cover most of me. I'd seen some pretty skimpy outfits at Callaghan's last Halloween. After that, we would go to Knightsbridge for the other events, formal festivities, and the wedding itself, which would take place at the local church in nine days' time. My flight home was on the seventeenth, giving me one day to relax after everything was over.

I hadn't contacted Ken, still not sure whether I should do so. If I didn't, would it hurt him? That wasn't what I wanted either. I'd told him I was coming, so I should at least be polite enough to call. After all, being polite went hand-in-hand with being Canadian, but since I would have so little free time, I wasn't sure I could even arrange to see him.

The plane stopped moving, and the seatbelt sign went off. I stood, grabbed my small bag from the overhead compartment, placed my messenger bag over my shoulder, and followed the rest of the Business Class passengers off the plane, heading towards the baggage claim and customs.

It didn't take long to find my blue swirl-patterned suitcase, and the customs agent was accommodating and friendly.

"Enjoy your stay."

I grinned. "I certainly hope so."

Following the signs, I headed towards the exit. The doors swished open. One look ahead of me, and I burst out laughing. Marley was impossible to miss. She wore a red dress and carried a huge bouquet from which protruded several small Union Jacks, the UK flag. When she saw me, she started waving the bouquet, endangering the life of everyone around her. I hurried in her direction before she could put out someone's eye. Careful not to crush the blooms, I hugged her, swallowing my tears.

"Marley, you look great. I've missed you so much. Seeing you online just isn't the same as in person. You look wonderful. You're glowing."

Her smile widened and her hazel eyes brimmed with tears. "I've missed you, too. It's been *so* long." She stressed the word as if it had a dozen o's in it. "Mom said you'd lost too much weight, but I think you look smashing." She chuckled. "That shade of blue brings out your eyes. I expected you to show up in a t-shirt, ripped jeans, and your work boots, with your hair all matted from trying to sleep on the plane."

I scrunched up my nose and shrugged. I wasn't offended since that was exactly what I would've looked like had Rachel and Bridget not gotten on my case. Between them, they'd given me a mild makeover. I'd drawn the line at hair lifts, color, and most cosmetics, but I agreed to a tinted moisturizer, mascara, and lipstick in a pearly peach shade. In addition to the suit I wore, my suitcase was full of new clothes including a couple of dresses—I refused to believe I would need six. I also had new underwear, a robe, slippers, and three nightgowns since I couldn't embarrass Marley in front of the staff by wearing my old, gungy stuff. I'd also brought my favorite sandals and two pairs of heels ... not the hooker kind, but higher than I was used to. I'd practiced walking in them and prayed I wouldn't fall on my face when the time came. At the moment, I wore shoes with wedge soles ... not fancy but comfortable enough assuming I wasn't planning on hiking anywhere. I had my running shoes for those times when I just had to run to clear my head or settle my nerves.

"I'll take that as a compliment. I figured I needed to step up my wardrobe a bit. It's not every day one's sister becomes a peer of the realm."

Marley gave me the once-over before handing me the flowers. "I like what you did to your hair, too." I'd had it trimmed and layered so that it looked fuller. I could still wear it in a ponytail for work. "These are for you. They're from Aaron. He feels awful that he can't be here to welcome you himself."

"They're lovely." Hopefully, they would last until we left for the country. In my opinion, there was nothing sadder than a vase full of wilted flowers.

"Let's get out of here," she said, relieving me of my large bag. "The car's over in reserved parking, but since the airport is so large, we're still quite far away."

I glanced down at her feet. As usual, she wore heels high enough to give me nosebleeds. How far did she expect to walk in those?

We'd only gone a few yards when I saw the moving sidewalk, essentially a flat escalator. She stepped onto it, pulling my bag up close to her. Warily, I did the same.

"I have so much to tell you. It's amazing how many Canadians are here. Did you know Ken Atchison was in England?"

"I did," I admitted, ignoring the fact that Karen was here, too. "Ken and I had dinner and drinks at the end of May, just before he moved here. He'll be in Newcastle for six months. I was going to see if we could get together while I'm here, but the schedule you sent is a busy one. Ken and I had a good time, and it'll be great to see him again."

Maybe that was a bit of a white lie, considering the secret still between us, but it could be fun—as long as it didn't get serious.

"That's wonderful news. I hadn't considered it since I always thought you despised the man, but the two of you would make a cute couple. I've solved your problem. I've invited them to the masquerade ball here in London and to the wedding."

"Them?"

"Karen and Ken. I couldn't very well ask one without the other. He must've told you she was here, too. Are you going deaf like Dad? I swear he only hears half of what you say to him. I met Ken in Harrods about a month ago, and he mentioned Karen was nursing here. Then, as luck would have it, I ran into her when I took Louis, the ambassador's son, to the Emergency Room a couple of weeks ago. He fell out of the apple tree behind the embassy. Thankfully, it was just a sprained wrist. Karen explained that she'd moved here with Billie Connors and April Green just before the pandemic."

I followed Marley from one moving sidewalk to another, admiring the busy, and surprisingly modern airport, barely listening to her as she droned on about the Despicable Three: Karen, Billie, and April, the girls who'd made my life miserable for so many years. I had no desire to do lunch or tea with any of them, and if Marley had such an outing planned, I'd invent a reason to bail. The terrible trio of spoiled, prissy bitches had always made me feel inadequate. They'd done their best to keep me on the outside of things, never letting me be part of the group. Was it any wonder I'd chosen to do the opposite of whatever they had? But I loved my life, and I refused to sit there and listen to them say or do anything that would make me feel inadequate this time. Just because Marley had invited them to the wedding didn't mean I had to socialize with them. I was pretty damn sure they wouldn't want to spend their time with me—especially not when there would be some unattached, rich, titled men around.

And then there was the truth about that night to consider. Why hadn't Karen told Ken what had happened? That was a mystery I would have to unravel for my peace of mind.

"It'll be nice for you to have some old friends around," her sister continued.

Four years younger than me, I hadn't realized that Marley hadn't understood the hell my life had been until now. Friends? Those harpies had been anything but my friends. Even Ken had been afraid of their sharp tongues and claws.

"You've always been a loner, uncomfortable in crowds, so I hope having people you know around will help you enjoy yourself. Mom and Dad had a look at my portion of the guest list, and they're happy with it."

I squared my shoulders. If Mom, Dad, and Marley were happy, I would be, too. This was her big day, and I wouldn't do anything to ruin it. I followed her onto yet another moving sidewalk.

Just how big was this airport? By now, my back and legs ached, my feet were killing me, and I was itchy from one end to the other, something that always happened when I was overtired. To add to my misery, I had to pee. We were nearing the end of another of them when I noticed the universal sign for a woman's washroom over on the left. Halleluia!

"When we get off this, can we make a quick detour? I *really* need to go."

"Sure. I forgot that for you, breakfast consists of half-a-dozen cups of coffee. Hazel makes a great cuppa. You won't miss your java each morning."

I wasn't sure who Hazel was, but I figured I'd put a face to the name soon enough. Maybe she was the barista at the coffee shop nearest Marley's apartment.

"Good to know."

Talking about any kind of liquid wasn't the conversation I needed, so as soon as we stepped off the conveyor belt, I handed her my carry-on and the flowers and rushed into the bathroom, grateful to find an empty stall. Once I started, I wasn't sure I would ever stop, but eventually, I did, no doubt to the joy of the other women waiting in line for my cubicle. I wiped with the thinnest, most useless toilet tissue I'd ever used and then washed and dried my hands before returning to the hallway. Onward and upward. Let's get the rest of the show on the road.

CHAPTER FIVE

Coming out of the washroom through a different door than the one I'd entered, I was disoriented, finding myself farther from my sister than expected. Marley was talking to someone. He was facing away from me, but they seemed to be good friends. He said something, she laughed, and then he hugged her, before heading back the way we'd come.

I walked over to her, ready to ask who that was when she handed me my bag and flowers and crossed to the people mover once more.

"There you are. This is the last one." She moved so quickly that three people managed to step between us, making it impossible to talk. If I didn't know better, I would swear she was avoiding me.

When I finally stepped off the moving sidewalk, I felt like someone who'd been too long away from solid ground. My knees were rubbery, but that could be an after-effect of flight or jetlag. It wasn't as if I was used to any of this.

"The car's just over this way." She hurried toward the exit.

"Who were you talking to while I was in the bathroom?" I had to run to keep up with her.

She turned and reddened, a sure sign that whatever she was about to say would either be a lie or something I didn't like—maybe both.

"I wasn't talking—"

"Marley, for heaven's sake. I saw you talking to him. He hugged you. I'm not trying to pry, but he ... he seemed familiar...."

She huffed out a breath and shook her head, her lips pursed. That strange sense of impending disaster gripped me, and I swallowed the sudden lump in my throat.

"I didn't want to tell you yet, but I suppose you would've found out soon enough. That was Zak Mitchum. He accompanied Crimson to Knightsbridge last week and went back for Briar Rose. Actually, he came in on the cargo plane just before you did. We wanted to be sure he would be here for the race and the wedding."

Time and I stood still, blocking the exit. A man jostled me on his way by.

"Whoa! Who the hell are Crimson and Briar Rose, and what do they and Zak have to do with your wedding?"

"Keep moving," a security man snapped. "You're blocking the exit."

Momentarily distracted, I started walking again, making sure to keep up with Marley.

"Answer me, Kid. What do those names and Zak have to do with the wedding, and don't you dare lie to me."

She huffed the way she always had when called onto the carpet.

"Fine. Zak's been looking after Aaron's horses at Cedar Glen, that's what he named his stud ranch. Crimson is a three-year-old who'll be racing next week. Briar Rose is a pregnant mare. When she foals, the newborn will belong to Knightsbridge. The foal and Crimson are gifts from Aaron to his brother who owns a racing stable there, a thank you for being his Best Man. Don't worry, I got you something more practical than a couple of horses." She laughed.

I wasn't amused. When I didn't comment, she continued.

"Aaron hired Zak to look after his animals four years ago when he bought the ranch. Since then, they've become fast friends. As Zak was accompanying the horses to England and will be helping them settle at Knightsbridge, the least we can do is invite him to be part of our wedding celebration, especially since he'll be there. For God's sake, don't look at me like that. It's not a disaster or anything."

My jaw gaped open. Disaster? This was more than a disaster. It was a mind-blowing, soul-destroying catastrophe along the lines of a meteor striking Earth and obliterating the dinosaurs. What was I going to do now?

I stared at my sister as if she'd suddenly developed a third eye in the center of her forehead.

And when were you going to tell me this? I wanted to scream.

Instead, I fisted my hand under the flowers and tried to keep my voice level. "I see. And while your fiancé was getting all chummy with his veterinarian, did you bother to mention to him that Zak and I had been engaged?"

"Of course. He asked me why you'd broken it off. Since I had no idea—I still don't—he asked Zak about it." She rolled her eyes. "Zak's comment was as noncommittal as yours. Irreconcilable differences or some such nonsense. He wouldn't elaborate, but that's more than you said, so I assume that you screwed up and ... well, it doesn't matter. Now, let's hurry. The Duchess is waiting for us."

Once more, I stopped in my tracks. I had not screwed up, Zak had, but at least his lackluster answer didn't embarrass either of us. It was her other words that set off all the alarms in my head.

"What do you mean, the Duchess? I thought we were going to your place. I'm not ready to mingle with the royals just yet. At the very least, I need to shower and change." And try to get my head around the fact that Zak would be at the wedding.

Marley laughed. "As if your appearance has ever made any difference to you. You're fine, and we'll be *en famille*. There's nothing formal about it, and it is my place. I live in Renfield House now. I was renting a one-bedroom flat. The lease expired a month ago, and there was no need to keep it. Since the Duke and Duchess have given us the house as a wedding present and will be moving to the country now that Jacob, the heir to the title, has taken his father's place in Parliament, I moved in early. With the pandemic over, they intend to travel once more. When they come to London, they'll be more than welcome to stay in the house. It does have eight bedrooms, or they could opt to stay with Jacob and Solange at their estate, Mayfield, just outside of the city. Elise enjoys seeing the grandchildren. Emily is seven, Imogene is five, Celine is two, and Solange just announced that she's expecting again. She's ten years younger than Jacob and they're hoping for a boy to carry the title."

"If the house in town has eight bedrooms, just how many bedrooms does Knightsbridge have?" Her home sounded more like a hotel than a house. I thought back to the little bungalow I'd loved in Cedar Lake. That three-bedroom ranch was all the house I wanted.

"It's a restored castle that's been in the family for centuries, originally gifted to them by King Henry VIII when he first ascended the throne, and the family has stayed on the right side of the Monarchy ever since. There are eighteen bedrooms in the main house and another four in the dowager house where I'll be staying until after the wedding. Mom and Dad, you, me, and Zak will stay there, but meals and such will all be at the main house. The guests who aren't invited to stay in the castle will have accommodations in the nearby villages. Tetbury's in the Cotswold district in Gloucestershire. King Charles and Queen Camilla have a home in the area as do many nobles."

Once again, I stopped walking. I wasn't sure what concerned me most, but at this rate, we might never make it to the car. Jogging and accidentally coming across the king and queen were one thing, but Zak not only attending the wedding but sleeping in the same house was something else.

"Are you telling me that Zak Mitchum is going to be staying in the same house as me? That I'm going to have to put up with him for the week until your wedding day? What other disastrous news have you been keeping from me? Let me guess. He's part of the wedding party. Seriously, Marley. How could you keep this from me?"

"Because I knew you'd overreact when you found out about it."

"Overreact? Do you think this is overreacting? I haven't even begun to overreact." My voice got louder with each statement.

She rolled her eyes. "Calm down, Marissa. You're attracting attention. Paparazzi are everywhere."

As if I gave a rat's ass about the paparazzi. Calm down? Had telling someone to calm down ever worked?

I glanced around, noticing the odd looks people were giving me. Damn it. This was England. People didn't display their emotions—something about a stiff upper lip. Doing my best to rein in my fury, I fisted my hand tighter, feeling my nails cut half-moons into my palms.

"He's not part of the wedding party, but he *is* Aaron's special guest. As such, he'll be part of all the festivities at Knightsbridge. I'm not asking you to spend time with him. I simply expect you to be polite. Canadians are polite. It's our shtick. Surely that isn't asking too much?

The blood in my veins turned to ice. I hadn't laid eyes on Zak in five years, not since ... Now, not only was I supposed to share accommodations with him, I was expected to be polite to him? Polite to the man who'd broken my heart and had left it in tatters? That was like going up to someone with a nut allergy and handing them a piece of the most gorgeous almond cake in the world and saying to them, "It's okay. Go ahead and eat your fill. It'll only kill you once. It'll be fun." This wedding might well be the death of me.

"You don't know what you're asking." Even after all this time, the mere mention of his name turned me into a mess.

Blinded by the tears in my eyes—was the damn mascara waterproof?—I stumbled and would've fallen had Marley not grabbed me. Wouldn't that have been cute? Me, covered in dirt and dust, tracks of mascara running down my cheeks, curtsying to the Duchess of Habersham. Did I have to curtsy? I wasn't sure. Maybe a head bow would suffice. I should ask Marley, but given my emotional state and the frown she wore, this didn't seem to be the right time.

Marley rolled her eyes once more. "I know you're tired, but we're almost there." She fixed her gaze on me and frowned. "Are you crying? Seriously? Crying? Over what?" She held up her hands in confusion, her shoulders raised. Huffing out a breath, she continued. "And you call me a drama queen." She shook her head. "Fine. I should've mentioned that Zak would be here as soon as I knew about it, but Rissa, this isn't like you. You're usually the cool, calm one. What was it Ken and some of the others called you? Oh yes, the Ice Queen."

Talk about hitting below the belt! My mouth opened and closed as I gasped for air and something to say, but she cut me off.

"You aren't, of course. You're the kindest, most caring person in the world, but you do tend to act rather than react—like running away from Cedar Lake without a reason. I'm sure your current hyper-emotional state is a result of jetlag. Once you get your circadian rhythm reestablished, you'll be your old self again."

"Easy for you to say," I mumbled. Since when was she an expert on circadian rhythm and jetlag?

"Look. I get it; I may not understand it, but I get it. You and Zak parted on what had to have been lousy terms, but you can't let one bad relationship ruin your life. I'll make sure you're not seated near him at any of the formal meals, and you can find a way to avoid him at the other functions. There will be dozens of people there. It's the best I can do. It's been five years. You've moved on—hell, you've left all of us in your dust—I'm sure he has, too. Whatever he may have done hurt you badly, but it isn't as if he left you standing at the altar, humiliating you in front of the whole town or anything."

My cheeks flamed. What he had done had been far, far worse, but unless I was willing to fess up to it, no one would understand. It wasn't just the fact that he'd cheated on me; it was that he'd cheated on me with Karen. If Ken were to be believed, Zak hadn't moved on. So what was I supposed to do?

The anger and frustration in Marley's voice came through loud and clear, eating at my conscience. This was her time, her big moment, and I was making it all about me.

"You're the one who broke it off," she went on. "If anyone should be upset about this situation, don't you think it should be him? You dumped him, and he told Aaron that you never even explained why. You never answered a single one of his calls, and we all know that you left town as if the devil himself had set your ass on fire. Mom and Dad were worried sick—so was I."

She stopped beside a silver sedan, turned toward me, her feet planted, her hands on her hips.

"We all were. Now, unless you're going to tell me what happened between you and why he shouldn't be here, you're going to have to come to grips with this. Aaron likes him, and I love Aaron. I love you, too, Rissa, but don't make me choose between you."

I shook my head, swallowed my pain and pride, sniffled since I didn't have a tissue—I never did when I needed one—and swiped away the tears, grateful to see that there were no black streaks on my fingers.

"I would never do that to you, Marley. You're right. I'm not myself. I've been carrying this around long enough. Maybe it's time Zak and I had a heart-to-heart talk about that night. If nothing else, it'll clear the air. It's time to let it go. It's no big deal ... like falling off a bicycle. Once you get back on again, you don't know why you made such a fuss about it in the first place." Of course in my case, that fall had left me broken-hearted and emotionally crippled for life. "I'm nothing if not resilient. Once I see Zak, I'll realize that none of it matters anymore. It was much ado about nothing as Shakespeare would say."

And if I die in my sleep, I'm going straight to hell for that one.

If you wanted to make yourself feel better, you told the truth; if you wanted to make someone else feel better, you told them what they wanted to hear. A white lie could erase a lot of pain—but a lie was still a lie, and eventually, the lies caught up with you. The road to hell was paved with good intentions.

Marley grinned. "There's the big sister I've missed. Two weeks today, you'll stand beside me when I marry the man I love." She opened the trunk and placed my suitcase inside, adding my carry-on bag. "Rissa, I never expected that my life would turn out this way. I want you to be as happy as I am."

"I promise to be as happy as I can," I lied, knowing I would be wallowing in misery until I got back to Brockton and for months, maybe even years after that.

It would take every bit of acting ability that I possessed to pull this off ... the problem was that I was no better at acting than at singing, and I sucked at that. I'd been in third grade when the children's choir director had taught me to lip-sync.

With the flowers still clutched in my arms, I went around to the passenger door, ready to face my uncertain future.

Marley followed me, stood aside, and chuckled.

I frowned. "What's so funny now?"

"Sorry, Sis. I know you can do anything you set your mind to, but while you may be able to drive here, at the moment you're tired. If that isn't enough, you don't know your way around."

I frowned. Drive? Who said I wanted to drive? I didn't even know where we were, let alone where we were going. I looked inside the car and shook my head. There was the steering wheel.

"Duh! Maybe I am suffering from jetlag," I snorted in my most unladylike manner. "I'd forgotten you drive on the left here."

"It's no biggie, and your Ontario driver's license is valid, so you can drive, but let's give you a day or two to get acclimated, shall we? The traffic won't be too bad since we're almost beyond what passes for a rush hour here, but it'll still be bloody miserable in places. You'll want to practice a bit on the back roads before you tackle London. The roundabouts can be a bitch if you get in the wrong lane."

In my mind, I was in the movie *European Vacation*, trapped in the car with Clark Griswold, caught in the Lambeth Bridge Roundabout, unable to get back into traffic. Chevy Chase had been on his way to their hotel from Heathrow. How many times had they passed Buckingham Palace? The odds were we would pass through that roundabout, too. I shuddered.

"Definitely need practice."

I hurried around to the left, got into the vehicle, and put on my seatbelt.

Marley started the car and pulled away from the curb.

For the next hour, Marley expertly navigated first a highway and later city streets, complete with roundabouts. As she did, occasionally pointing out landmarks, she talked about her life at the embassy, the various charities Aaron and his family supported, the British affection for football, known to us as soccer, and countless other things that went in one ear and out the other. My brain was too tired and confused to store anything that might be important, and I'm sure she knew it since she also avoided mentioning Zak and the wedding.

She stopped at a pedestrian crossing to let a busload of tourists following a man with an umbrella cross the road. Who did he think he was? Mary Poppins?

"That's Kensington Park," she indicated an area to the right, "and you can see Kensington Palace, the official London residence of the Prince and Princess of Wales and their children. If you like, you can tour it and Buckingham Palace while you're here. Just say the word, and I'll make the arrangements. I have some things to do at the embassy, but we can work around those. You have to see the Tower of London—that's where Aaron and I met—Big Ben, and the London Eye. The view from the top is magnificent."

"I'll bet it is," I agreed, although the thought of being more than four hundred feet above ground in nothing but a flimsy capsule made me queasy. I wasn't afraid of heights. I was afraid of falling and landing on the pavement, my body smashed like a damn bug against a windshield.

"We could do it tomorrow. Our first visit to Madame Denise, the dressmaker is the day after, and then we have an appointment to look at hats and stuff. People may rarely wear hats at home, but here they're often quite necessary, especially when we go to the horse race on Sunday, Baroness Kingsford's garden party on Monday—it's an unofficial wedding shower for me—the polo match Tuesday, and the gymkhana on Wednesday."

I frowned. "What's a gymkhana?" The word was vaguely familiar.

"It's an equestrian event with speed pattern racing and timed games for riders on horses. The local Pony Club is hosting one, and Emily and Imogene usually compete. Celine isn't old enough yet. Back home, we just called them country fairs. You used to be quite good at dressage."

"That seems like a lifetime ago. I haven't been on a horse in more than five years."

"There are several good riding mounts at Knightsbridge. I'm sure Leon, who's in charge of the stables, can find one suitable for you. Where was I? Oh yes, our final fitting is Thursday morning—Madame Denise and her staff will come to the country for it. Knightsbridge is two hours from London. So, everything here kicks off with the opera on Friday. There's a garnet cocktail dress in your room for that. I picked it out for you. If it needs any adjustments, Clara can take care of it."

My brain woke up. "Who's Clara?"

"She's the Duchess's assistant. She looks after whatever needs doing."

"Like a lady's maid?" I had visions of the elderly woman, resembling Queen Victoria at her Diamond Jubilee, standing there while some woman in a dreary maid's uniform tied her bra.

"No. Her job is a lot like mine at the embassy. She arranges things, sets the Duchess's calendar so that there aren't any conflicts, and accompanies Her

Grace when necessary. I'll be keeping her on to help me when the time comes."

I cocked my head and shifted in the seat. Marley loved working as a diplomat. Was she planning to quit?

"Are you going to keep working at the embassy after you get back from your honeymoon?"

Marley smiled and nodded. "I will but only until my contract ends in November. I'll train the new assistant who'll be working with a new ambassador. I'll pitch in if they need me in an emergency. Jameson Bolt's term is over then, and he and his family are returning to Canada. You'll meet him since he and Louisa are coming to the masquerade as well as the wedding. In January, I'll take over some of Aaron's charity work as well as his mother's. With another baby on the way, Solange can't do it. I'll probably end up with some of hers, too."

"I see." Hobnobbing with the rich and famous would suit Marley who was dignity and political correctness personified, while I would go crazy without something hands-on to do. "Sounds like you'll have your hands full."

"I hope so. Renfield House isn't far from here," she continued. "I assume you still jog, and this is a great place to do it, although we have an excellent gym inside the house. Until you know your way around, you might want to ask one of the staff to join you. There are a few who run. It's safe enough here, but..." She shrugged. "Reynolds usually goes out with Aaron when he wants to jog."

The idea of running with a bodyguard—no matter what she called it that's what it was— seemed weird to me. But then again, I was an electrician from Brockton, not a peer who was actually in the top forty in line for the throne. Of course, with each new baby born to those ahead of him, he got farther behind. Take Princess Anne. She'd gone from being fourth behind her brothers to seventeenth now.

Before I could figure out how to argue the need for an escort, the last of the doddering tourists stepped onto the sidewalk, and the traffic started moving again. There were probably more cars on this street right now than in the whole of Brockton.

Marley drove a few more blocks and then signaled a right turn, stopping in front of massive wrought iron gates. She pressed a button on the sun visor, and the gates opened. I could see the red brick mansion from here.

"That's your house?" I gulped. "It's ... it's huge. Has Mom seen this place?"

Marley laughed. "She has. I took her to meet the Duke and Duchess the first time they were here, just after we announced our engagement. She was quite impressed, but you know Mom. She wanted to know how many people it took to keep it clean and wash all the windows. The answer is eight full-time, as well as a chauffeur, and a dozen part-timers who work both here and at Knightsbridge depending on the time of year. With the Duke and Duchess moving there permanently, I'll probably have to hire more staff for here. If there's a special function, like the masquerade ball we're hosting here on Saturday evening, we hire specifically for the occasion. While the Duke and Duchess rarely drive in the city anymore, Aaron likes to take his car during the day as do I. In the evenings, we use the chauffeur. This car was one of my engagement gifts. There were also a few pieces of jewelry and my ring, of course."

She'd shown me the ring in one of our video chats, and I glanced at it now. The square-cut emerald surrounded by diamonds was big enough to choke a horse.

"Some gift. All I got was a ring which I threw back at him." I didn't mention that I had the ring again, nor the fact that I'd brought it with me. Not knowing Zak would be here, I'd planned to wear it to avoid unwanted attention. Now, I would welcome any attention from anyone but him.

As we approached the house, I noticed the impressive lawns. It would take a day just to cut that grass and weed those fancy flowerbeds. Of course, with my experience, I would kill off all the greenery in no time—some silly rule about watering more than once a month.

"Whoever does the gardening around here must be on great terms with Mother Nature. Your lawn looks as good as most golf courses."

She chuckled. "I'll tell Evans that you said so. He tends to each of those plants as if they were his children. The first time Aaron took me here, I was in shock. I knew he wasn't a pauper, but I hadn't expected anything like this. That's when he explained his pedigree. The title is hereditary and can only be inherited by a direct male descendant. If anything were to happen to Jacob, unless he and Solange have a son this time, the title will pass to Aaron. The house was built in the mid-eighteen hundreds, but it's been consistently modernized and upgraded."

"Impressive." That was an understatement. From the outside, I could see that the three-story house with a mansard roof was massive. "So you could end up being a duchess?"

"I don't know. Aaron thinks the Duke should approach King Charles and asked that the rule be changed, like the way Queen Elizabeth changed the rules of succession so that Princess Charlotte is next in line behind Prince George, making it age and not gender."

I nodded. "Makes sense. The world has moved beyond male dominance in a lot of things." I examined the house. "I know you mentioned eight bedrooms, but just how big is this place?"

"Well, each bedroom has its own bathroom. In addition, there are three guest water closets ... what they call powder rooms here, three reception rooms, two offices, a library, a formal and an informal dining room, a kitchen, a lift servicing all floors, a conservatory full of exotic plants—the Duke raises orchids out in the country—three storage rooms, two utility rooms, a gymnasium, as well-equipped as any you'll ever find, a sauna, a hot tub, and a swim spa. Then, out back you'll find the annex housing the servant quarters, the four-car garage, and the private walled garden and sitting area, what you'd call a deck. There isn't an outdoor pool here, but there's an Olympic-sized one in the country. Oh, and the butler and cook have an apartment off the kitchen. At the moment, there should be men out there setting up a tent for Saturday night."

"Wow!" That was the only word I could think of. I'd been to hotels and resorts with fewer amenities.

A butler, a cook, and a chauffeur? As I'd said, impressive. I would be thrilled to be able to afford a cleaning lady once every couple of weeks.

CHAPTER SIX

Marley stopped the car in front of the house. As if he'd been peeking through the window awaiting our arrival, a gray-haired man in his late forties, wearing a dark, three-piece suit, opened the door and came down the stairs. Had I just walked into a game of *Clue*? If there were a murder committed here tonight, it would be easy to believe who'd done it—the butler, in the hall, with a candlestick ... or a revolver, or a knife. In fact, any of the weapons would do.

I frowned. Was he wearing an earpiece like a Secret Serviceman? Since when did butlers do that?

He opened Marley's door and held out his hand to help her out.

"Thanks, James. I didn't expect to see you here. I thought you'd be gone by now."

Not the butler. Maybe the chauffeur?

"His Grace decided to wait to greet your sister. He and the Duchess are in the conservatory. I'll have Reynolds take the luggage to Miss Marissa's room." He hurried around to my door and opened it, reaching for the flowers. "Welcome to Renfield House." He smiled, changing his forbidding appearance from terrifying to simply scary. "I'll have Kelsey put these in water and take them up to your room."

"Thank you," I mumbled.

I handed him the bouquet and got out of the car, grateful that my legs weren't quite as rubbery as they'd been. I was going to face not only the Duchess but the Duke. Suddenly, I needed to pee again. I always did when I got nervous. Since I was going to be a pack of nerves while I was here, maybe I should consider acquiring incontinency underwear.

"I'll take her to them, James. Thanks. Come on." Marley led the way into the house. On the right was a staircase with a beautifully carved banister. Ornate antiques, gleaming silver, and paintings that weren't reproductions lined the hall. The last time I'd seen this much highly polished wood had been in church. As we walked along, I glanced into formal rooms where the doors were open, catching sight of a person dusting. It must take forever to clean this place.

Marley turned the corner and opened a set of double doors. It was like stepping into the Garden of Eden. I could hear birds and running water. Over on the left, sitting on cushioned chairs and sipping what I hoped was coffee but was probably tea, sat a couple who didn't look at all like the people I'd imagined. I'd been thinking along the lines of an elderly couple, and while the Duke and Duchess might be older than Mom and Dad, they certainly weren't in their dotage. I should've taken the time to look them up ... I'd been planning to, but every time I'd started, something had interrupted me.

Roderick Sykes, Duke of Habersham, might be in his seventies, given that Aaron was thirty-eight and his brother a few years older, but he certainly didn't look his age. He had what I could only describe as Friar Tuck hair—gray on the sides but bald on top—and a trimmed mustache, reminding me of Sean Connery. The Duke wore dark-rimmed glasses but his gray eyes sparkled with animation. Like James, he wore a dark three-piece suit with a white shirt and a striped tie. Beside him, in a gorgeous aquamarine caftan that must've come straight off the runway in Paris was a woman with silver hair and the quintessential English rose complexion.

He glanced up when the door opened and smiled. "There you are, Marley. This lovely lady must be your sister. You described her perfectly." He stood and extended his hand.

I froze. What was I supposed to do? Kiss his ring? He wasn't a bishop or the Pope. Good manners instilled in me by my mother came to my rescue. I stepped forward and reached for his hand, shaking it quickly and then releasing it.

"Your Grace. It's very nice to meet you. You have a beautiful home. Thanks for letting me stay here."

He smiled. "No thanks required, young lady. This is your sister's home. We're pleased to welcome her and you to the family. This is my wife, Elise."

The Duchess of Habersham stood. She was younger than her husband with gorgeous aquamarine eyes sparkling behind light-framed glasses. Her hair was styled in a fashion similar to what Queen Elizabeth had worn. She moved toward me before I could react.

"Marissa, it's a pleasure to meet you," she began before pulling me into a hug. "We both hope you'll feel at home here and at Knightsbridge."

My pulse raced as I awkwardly reciprocated the embrace. Didn't the book say you weren't supposed to touch royalty? It didn't say anything about what you were supposed to do if they touched you first. You could probably get away with shaking hands but hugging?

When she released me, I stepped back. It was a little late to try to curtsy now.

"Your Grace, it's my pleasure to meet you as well. Marley speaks highly of you." She hadn't said all that much, but what she had said had all been positive.

"Join us. At home like this, we don't use formalities. Please call us Roderick and Elise."

I nodded, doing my best to appear cool and confident when I was a mass of nerves.

"Of course. But if I put my foot in my mouth or do something gauche, I hope you'll forgive me." How had Marley ever managed to get comfortable with all of this?

Elise smiled. "You'll be fine. And don't worry about the rest of the family. We aren't as stuffy as people think."

The Duke and Duchess resumed their seats. Marley settled on the chair next to the Duke, and I sat between her and the Duchess. I seemed to have my act together—at least I was breathing normally—until a voice spoke behind me, and I jumped.

"What the—" I swallowed the expletive when Marley kicked me. Where the hell had that woman come from?

"What would you like to drink, Marissa?" The Duchess didn't comment on my startled expression. No doubt she was used to having people sneak up on her. "Roderick and I are having tea, but feel free to ask for whatever you'd like—juice, coffee, chocolate, or whatever else you'd prefer."

How about a double shot of whiskey?

"Coffee," I managed to choke out.

"I'll have coffee, too, Megan, and can you bring some of your mother's scones and jam? I skipped breakfast to make sure to get to the airport on time."

"Yes, Ma'am." The smiling girl turned and retraced her steps moving so soundlessly that I checked to make sure her feet were touching the ground—they were.

I sat back admiring the room, looking up now and then to see if the birds I heard were real or white noise, not sure what to do with my hands. The running water from a fountain hidden somewhere in the room was soothing but presented another problem.

Unable to control my bladder much longer, I leaned over to Marley. "Did you mention water closets earlier? I'd like to wash my hands before the coffee and scones get here."

Marley smiled, the sparkle in her eyes telling me she knew exactly what I wanted. "Go out the conservatory doors, and it's the first door on the left."

I nodded and turned to my hosts. "If you'll excuse me, I'll be right back."

I hurried out of the room, grateful to find the door without getting lost. Now if I could find my way back...

When I returned, the coffee and scones had been delivered.

"How was your flight?" Elise asked.

"Incredible," I answered truthfully. "I've never flown Business Class before. It's very different from Economy."

Duh! As if a Duchess would know what flying economy was like! Still, since she seemed interested, I described the meals and the other amenities I'd enjoyed. The Duchess spoke of her most recent flight to Japan and the problems she'd had with jetlag afterward. Since I didn't feel too tired, I considered myself lucky.

Without realizing it, I'd eaten two scones with butter and jam. The baked goods were to die for, and I could easily see myself putting on weight if I ate sweets like these every day. As Marley had promised, the coffee was the best I'd ever tasted. The Duke asked me questions about my job and my business, never making me feel inferior. He even asked me if I could have a look at the ceiling fan in one of his greenhouses at Knightsbridge. I was genuinely disappointed when he rose to excuse himself to go to the office. I didn't ask what he did, but it must have been important if a man his age and obvious wealth was still working.

After he left, the conversation turned to matters concerning the coming ball, and while I tried to focus, the dose of adrenalin I'd gotten earlier had worn off. My "constantly on the go back home" body was antsy. Sitting still was a chore, and try as I might, I simply couldn't follow the conversation. My eyes burned, and I yawned. I needed to get up and move or I would fall asleep on the spot. I twitched and jerked upright. Had I fallen asleep? With my luck, not only had I drooled, I'd probably snored.

The Duchess smiled. "You're tired, my dear, and that's to be expected. Marley, why don't you show Marissa to her room? We'll have a light lunch at one. Solange is coming by with the children. She has a doctor's appointment at three, and they'll stay here with me. I enjoy these quick visits."

One? What time was it now? I glanced at the clock on the wall. Ten-thirty, which would be five-thirty back home. No wonder I was tired. I would still be in bed if I were in Brockton.

I stood. "Thank you so much for making me feel welcome. I am tired, but I'm sure a shower will fix me right up. I look forward to meeting your daughter-in-law and her children."

Marley got to her feet. "Come on. I'll take you up. You'll like Solange, and the girls are precious. I'll see you at lunch, Elise."

I followed Marley back down the hall to another set of wooden doors that slid open when she pushed the call button on the wall. Inside the elevator or lift as they called it here, she pressed the button marked 3. Despite the coffee and the fact that I'd slept on the plane, I was tired and felt grubby. I might wear the same set of coveralls for a week, but I changed my underwear and what I wore under the overalls every day. These had gone way over the twenty-four-hour limit. I couldn't even vouch for the efficacy of my deodorant.

"God, I've never wanted a shower as much as I do now," I grumbled.

Marley laughed. "I'm sure you do. It's the first thing most of us want after a long flight. Once you clean up, you'll feel better. Have a snooze, but not a long one. The sooner you can get back to your regular sleep pattern the better."

I nodded. "I didn't expect them to be so normal. I was terrified that I'd put my foot in my mouth and embarrass you."

She smiled. "You could never do that. Roderick and Elise are just people when it comes right down to it. So are Solange and Jacob, and you're going to love Aaron. As he says, he puts on his pants, one leg at a time, like every other person on the planet. When he told me who and what he was, I called him a liar. He took out his passport to prove it." She shook her head. "Elise does a lot of charity work and the Duke has always been a people person. As Aaron puts it, they've moved with the times, accepting that society has changed. You'll meet your share of fuddy-duddies at the wedding and the garden party, but you'll also meet a lot who've come into the twenty-first century with their eyes open."

The elevator doors slid apart, and we stepped into a spacious hallway. She opened the door across from the elevator.

"I've put you in here this time. This floor used to be the nursery when Aaron and Jacob were younger. The Duchess had the two bedrooms redone into spacious suites. Until we have children, they're reserved for special guests."

I removed my suit jacket, revealing the blue and yellow top I'd worn under it, and dropped it on the foot of the bed.

The room, decorated in green and cream was larger than my apartment in Brockton. The furniture, clearly antique, was oak and had been polished to a high sheen. I'd never slept in a canopied bed with bed curtains before. It reminded me a little of the scene from *A Christmas Carol* where Scrooge was visited by the ghosts.

"Is this place haunted?" I blurted, hoping that any spirits would be benevolent ones.

Marley laughed. "You and your imagination. I suppose all houses over a hundred and fifty years old probably are, but if you're asking if I've ever seen a ghost, then the answer is no. Talk to Jeeves. He's the butler. He can tell you all about the house's history."

I frowned. "Jeeves? Then, who's James? I thought he was the butler."

She shook her head. "Nope. He's the Duke's bodyguard and assistant. Somedays, he also doubles as chauffeur if the Duchess needs the car and driver." She chuckled. "You look the way I expect Alice did when she went down the rabbit hole."

"It's a lot to get used to," I argued.

"I know. I'm just getting my head around some of it now. I can understand how overwhelmed Meghan must've felt with all of the rules she had to follow married to a prince who is fifth in line for the throne. She was a celebrity, but that pales in comparison to being a royal here in Britain. The paparazzi can be cruel and relentless. Aaron and I will be quite far down the pecking order, but that doesn't matter much to some of the so-called experts on royalty. We both know that I don't have a drop of blue blood, but once I become Lady Broadmere ... I had to get used to a lot of protocol working for the ambassador and while my life won't be quite as crazy as hers would've been had she and Harry not left England, it will have its share of rules and responsibilities. Now, let me show you around. You've got a walk-in closet, a sitting area, as well as your own bathroom. The Internet password should be in the top drawer of the desk. If there's anything you need, pick up the phone. It connects to the kitchen and someone will answer at any time of the day or night and send up whatever you need."

The servants must work shifts, but surely there wouldn't be a lot to do at night?

"Thanks. Good to know, but I'm sure I can manage." I would have to remember that wandering around the house at night looking for ice cream wouldn't be a good idea. I noticed the laptop on the desk. It looked a lot like mine.

Marley pulled open the drapes. "You've got a great view from here. You face east and should see some spectacular sunrises. There are only two bedrooms on this floor. The third room used to be a playroom and later a classroom. It's still full of toys, and the kids will probably come up here to play after lunch. The girls are sweet. Now, as for the rest of the accommodations, as I said, I'm next door. My window faces the back of the house. Aaron and his parents have rooms on the second floor and Mom and Dad will sleep down there when they arrive. At the moment, the master bedroom is being redone and should be finished by the time we get back from our honeymoon. I'm having my office attached to it. I can convert it into a nursery for the baby's first few months." She shrugged. "I just need to get pregnant."

The wistfulness in her voice was clear. I sighed. That had been my dream five years ago. Now, I doubted it would ever happen. That thought reminded me of Zak, and my good mood plummeted. Not wanting to upset Marley, I changed the subject. I needed some alone time to come to grips with all of this and what I'd learned earlier. I couldn't change any of it, but I needed to prepare myself for it ... psych myself up and hope for the best.

"This ... this is fantastic. I feel like a fairy princess." I noted that my cases hadn't been brought upstairs yet. Bummer! "I was hoping to shower and unpack."

"You don't have to unpack. Katie would've done it for you." She pulled open the drawer on the dresser. "See?"

There were my undergarments, all neatly put away, panties, bras, pantyhose, and socks. I'd heard of people with organized sock drawers—never thought I would be one of them. The second drawer revealed T-shirts, swimsuits, shorts, and my running gear, while my nighties were in the bottom one.

"That saves time," I joked, but I was grateful that everything that had been in the suitcase, including my running gear, was new or clean. "I'll have to thank her when I see her." I indicated the desk. "I suppose that is *my* laptop?"

"Probably. You'll find your empty bags in the closet. I know it's hard to imagine, but you do get used to having things done for you. It's quite nice. You can still look after yourself if you prefer, but Katie's a whizz with hair and makeup—not that you can't manage on your own."

I huffed out a breath. "If you say so, but you know me. All that girly stuff isn't my forte. I'm in the deep end here, and I don't know how to swim."

Marley sighed. "Just let things happen, Rissa. Go with the flow. Learn to tread water and float. You've fought for everything your entire life; now, for the next few days, take what's being offered and just enjoy it. Things will be back to normal for you in no time. Come on. Let me show you the dress you'll be wearing to the opera. The minute I saw it, I knew it was perfect for you. You can try it on after your shower."

She opened the door to the walk-in closet, and I followed her inside. I stopped. My dresses, slacks, tops, and skirts hung there. My shoes were on the shoe rack, but it was the dress hanging opposite them that captured my attention. It had to be the most beautiful dress I had ever seen. The tea-length, garnet chiffon had a halter neck, a fitted waist, and a full skirt. Beside it hung a matching jacket, that shimmered as if it were alive, and under it were coordinated sandals and a small clutch. I reached for the dress and held it in front of me, staring into the full-length mirror.

"It's beautiful, Marley. I don't know what to say. Even my prom dress wasn't that spectacular."

Hell, the wedding dress that still hung in my closet, a permanent reminder that love hurt, paled in comparison.

She smiled. "The look on your face says it all, and you're welcome. Now, why don't you shower? I'll have Megan bring up some coffee, and you can settle on the lounge and read or get caught up on your computer. I'm sure you have business emails to answer. I have a few calls to make for the embassy, but I'll meet you in the breakfast room at a quarter-to-one. Any of the staff can show you where it is. Once Solange leaves for her appointment, I'll give you the grand tour." She led me back into the bedroom. "I'll see you later."

"Wait," I cried. "What am I supposed to wear for lunch?"

"Whatever you like, although I don't recommend shorts. Breakfast and lunch are informal, but you'll need a dress or a skirt for dinner. I heard Hazel say she'd prepared a special menu in your honor."

I nodded. Hopefully, I wouldn't regain those kilos while I was here. If I did, I wouldn't have anything to wear—I'd never considered naked to be my best look.

Once she closed the door, I twirled around the room like a kid, bounced on the bed, grateful that while the frame might be antique, the mattress wasn't, and then kicked off my shoes. I went back into the closet—I'd seen my robe and slippers in there. I put my wedged-sole shoes on the shoe rack and headed into the bathroom. Even my toiletries had been unpacked and lined up on the shelf. Thick, green towels hung from a bar next to the walk-in shower. Beside it was a soaking tub. This bathroom was bigger than my bedroom back home.

Katie, whoever she was, had already placed my shampoo and conditioner in the shower. I stripped off my clothes, put them in what I assumed was a clothes hamper, and turned on the water. Stepping under the jets, I smiled. Life didn't get any better than this. It would all go to hell in a handbasket when Zak showed up, but for now, it was just about perfect.

When I felt the shower had sufficiently revived me, I turned off the water, wrapped myself in one of the bath sheets, and reached for the hairdryer. For the second time today, since I'd washed my face on the plane, I added moisturizer and lip gloss, omitting the mascara. Going into the bedroom, I found a carafe filled with fresh coffee sitting on the desk. I poured myself a cup, added cream and sugar, and settled at the computer.

I opened my emails. Just because I was away didn't mean I could ignore the business. I replied where I could and promised to contact others when I returned. Business completed, I wrote a detailed message to Bridget letting her know I'd arrived. After that email was sent, I opened my contacts, found the address I'd put in when I'd started to write to Ken but had changed my mind, and sent off a quick message.

Hi Ken, I've just arrived in the UK. Marley tells me you'll be at the masquerade and the wedding. I'm looking forward to seeing you. Marissa.

I read it several times. Should I add something about making plans for later? Should I mention Karen? I decided to leave it the way it was. The truth about that night was still out there. Marley was right, I did owe Zak an explanation, but so did

Karen. I wasn't looking forward to either of those confrontations.

I'd just poured myself another cup of coffee when the computer dinged, indicating I had mail. I opened my email program once more. It was from Ken.

Marissa, I've been waiting to hear from you. I'm looking forward to seeing you as well but we don't have to wait until the masquerade. I'll be arriving in London on Friday and will attend the supper after the opera. Couldn't get a ticket for the show itself. Keep a few spots open on your dance card for me. Love, Ken

I scrutinized the message. Was there an air of reprimand in his *I've been waiting to hear from you*, or was I imagining it out of my own guilt? Marley hadn't mentioned that he would be at the meal after the opera, or had that been one of the things I'd missed earlier in the conservatory? The dance was here at Renfield House. Would Karen be coming too? Would that be my chance to talk to her before Zak showed up at Knightsbridge? And what did he mean by *Love, Ken*?

My brain began to swirl with all kinds of complications I didn't need. Closing the computer, I settled back in the wingchair and sipped my coffee. He'd mentioned a dance card. I'd read enough Regency romances to know what that was. Thank God Zak wouldn't be here for that. Would he claim a slot on my dance card at the wedding? Would I even have one, or was Ken just being funny? There was no point in worrying right now. I set down the cup and closed my eyes.

* * *

I awoke to the sounds of police and ambulance sirens, the tone and stridency no different than the way they would've sounded back home. It took me a second to realize where I was, but once I did, I jumped up in a panic. Dressing quickly in my new jeans and a red T-shirt—Marley had said it was informal and both of these garments were new—I slipped my feet into my sandals, pulled my hair into a ponytail, added gold hoop earrings, and freshened my lip gloss. It was almost one by the time I made my way downstairs and found a servant who could show me the way to the breakfast room. Three women and three children were seated at the table.

"There you are, Marissa. I hope you're feeling rested," Elise asked, a welcoming smile on her face.

"I am, thank you. I hope I didn't keep you waiting."

I settled into the empty chair between the two little girls. The youngest was across from me in a highchair, seated between Marley and the woman I assumed was her mother.

"Not at all. Let me introduce you. The young lady on your left is Imogene and the one on your right is Emily. The one in the highchair is Celine and beside her is my daughter-in-law, Solange De la Forêt Sykes." She smiled. "Allow me to present, Marissa Kimble, Marley's sister. How would you like the children to address you?"

I blinked. "Marissa or Rissa is fine with me," I answered, taken aback. What else would they call me? "It's a pleasure to meet you all." It suddenly occurred to me that there would be a formal way to address them, but if there were, it wasn't mentioned.

Lunch was a selection of sandwiches with various fillings and condiments as well as a choice of crisps, which were potato chips, or a tossed salad. I opted for the salad and water, while the two older girls had crisps and juice. Celine ate cucumber slices and carrots with her crustless, minced ham sandwich. The simple meal and the small room with windows open to the backyard made me feel at home.

The conversation was lively with the girls talking about their new school. Solange, the daughter of a French Count, Louis De la Forêt whose wines were legendary, was a vivacious brunette in her mid-thirties. This might be her fourth pregnancy, but she was in great shape, obviously not suffering from morning sickness. The baby bump was there under her clothes, indicating she must be in her second trimester. The girls, dressed in coordinating tops and knee-length shorts, truly were angels, well-behaved and well-spoken.

As soon as the meal was over, Solange excused herself. She had to stop at the dressmaker's to have her gowns adjusted before going to the doctor's rooms. Elise and Megan took the children up to the playroom, while, as promised, Marley gave me a tour of the house.

The place was magnificent, and I couldn't deny being a little bit envious—all right, a whole lot envious, especially of the library—but while I wouldn't live here, I would get to visit.

"Honestly, on a day-to-day basis, we don't use much of the place. Other than the bedrooms, the breakfast room, the informal dining room, the small receiving room which you might call the family room since there's an entertainment system in there, and the conservatory as well as the kitchen and the gym area get the most use."

"The birds I heard this morning, were they real or just like elevator music?"

She chuckled. "Very real, although some of them will be moving to Knightsbridge with Roderick and Elise. Let me show you."

I followed her back into the conservatory and around the wall of plants to meet the caged birds I'd heard earlier. Did I say caged? I'd never seen anything like this. It was an enclosure with its own trees, as close to being loose and outdoors as any bird could get. The sounds of running water I'd heard earlier came from a miniature waterfall within their enclosure.

"They're called Tropical Parula and originated in Mexico." The tiny birds were blue with yellow heads. "Roderick raises them. He'll leave half a dozen here, but the rest will go with him."

"They're gorgeous. This has to be as close to paradise as anyone can get in the city. Other than my bedroom, this is the best room in the house."

At four, Elise and the girls joined us on the outside deck for tea, and Hazel outdid herself with cucumber sandwiches on pink bread, cut into circles and squares, tea cakes, biscuits, which I called cookies, as well as jams, and jellies. I couldn't believe I could eat again. I'd done more eating today than I had most days back in Brockton. I limited my food selection and settled back to enjoy my cup of Earl Grey tea.

CHAPTER SEVEN

Solange collected the girls at four-thirty and assured the Duchess that all had gone well at the obstetrician's office. Once she left, Hazel Brown, the cook, joined us and she, Marley, and Elise discussed the menus for the late supper the night of the masquerade. Megan came out to collect the dishes, and my brain latched onto an old Herman's Hermits song, "Mrs. Brown, You've Got a Lovely Daughter."

Needing exercise and to get away before I started humming and disgracing myself, I opted to take a walk around the grounds. I promised to stay within the gates, not that I envisioned anyone mistaking me for one of the aristocracy—the maid, perhaps, but definitely not a lady. I wasn't ready to go off exploring on my own at any rate, and I was certain the yard was plenty big enough to keep me busy. The colorful variety of flowers amazed me. I stood and watched the group of men putting up a circus tent for the overflow from the ball Saturday night. They were even laying down the wooden pallets that would create a floor. I couldn't begin to imagine the damage that would do to the beautiful lawn. When they packed it in for the day, I continued my perusal. Eventually, I found a quiet bench in a secluded corner of the garden and sat there enjoying the sounds of birds and bees as well as those of the city, some familiar like old friends, others new and exciting like this entire venture. The ding-donging of Big Ben indicated it was six and time to get ready for yet another meal.

Recalling Marley's admonition to get dressed for dinner, I pulled my hair into a knot at the back of my head in what passed for a sophisticated look for me, donned pantyhose although I despised them, and pulled on a knee-length emerald green swing dress that was both cool and comfortable. Finally, I slipped on the black heels I'd purchased just for the occasion. Going into the bathroom, pleased that I wasn't wobbling too badly, I washed my face and redid the tinted moisturizer, adding a little of the mascara Bridget had convinced me I needed and the peach lipstick. The gold hoop earrings Mom had given me at Christmas added the final touch to my appearance. I hadn't been this fancied up in years.

At seven, I made my way to the smallest of the receiving rooms, the one that doubled as a family room. That was when I realized that what I considered dressed up, wasn't dressed up at all.

The Duchess stood next to Marley, her tea-length beige chiffon dress the kind of thing I would expect to see the night of the opera, not for dinner alone at home. The amber necklace and earrings she wore had to have cost a small fortune. Beside her, Marley wore an above-the-knee, deep blue, V-necked satin gown that hugged her curves. Her curly hair was pulled to the side and held in place by a sapphire clip that matched her earrings and necklace. Even the Duke was dressed to the nines, sporting a white dinner jacket and black pants, resembling an aging James Bond. I swallowed my trepidation and stepped into the room.

Take it or leave it. This is the best I've got.

"Marissa, don't you look lovely," the Duke said, an appreciative gleam in his eyes. "Would you care for an Aperol Spritz?"

Thrown off-guard by the genuine welcome, I nodded. "That sounds interesting; I'll try one."

Within seconds, the man behind the bar was mixing the ingredients over ice—the bright orange Aperol liqueur, the Prosecco, the club soda, and garnishing it all with a slice of orange. He set the glass on a silver tray and carried it over to me.

"Madam." He presented the glass.

I reached for it. "Thank you." I sipped. "Delicious."

Marley came to stand beside me. "That color looks great on you. I can't wait to see you in the gowns Madame Denise has made for you."

"Thanks. I'm not as dressed up as you are—"

"You look fine. I told you, I would make sure you had everything you needed to fit in here, and I mean it," Marley interrupted. "I know this isn't your world, Rissa. That's why the fact that you're willing to step out of your comfort zone means so much to me. Now, how was your quiet time in the garden?"

"It was wonderful. There are so many different plants..."

By the time Jeeves announced dinner, I was relaxed and enjoying both the aperitifs and the conversation.

Seeing Marley's example, I set my empty glass on a coaster on a side table and followed the Duke and Duchess into the informal dining room with its table for twelve, although only one end of it was set. The Duke sat at the head of the table, the Duchess on his right, while I was placed on his left with Marley beside me. The table glistened with silver and crystal, and my nerves took hold of me once more.

Concerned about my lack of table etiquette, I glanced down in relief. This place setting had only two knives, two forks, two spoons, and half of the glassware and cutlery above the plate that I expected. I smiled. I had this.

Jeeves appeared with a wine bottle and poured a small amount into the Duke's white wine glass. When he approved it, the butler who was also the sommelier, added slightly to his glass and then came around and did the same to ours.

"This wine is from Solange's father's winery," the Duke explained, raising his glass. "Welcome to Britain, Marissa."

No one clinked glasses the way they would've back home, but we all raised them, smiled at each other, and took a sip.

"Thank you, and the wine is delicious." I wished the man had poured more into my glass.

The door opened and a server came in, carrying the first course.

The cream of something green soup was served in bowls with small handles on each side. I waited until everyone was served and then reached for the same spoon they had. From the steam rising from the bowls, it was obvious that the soup was hot. Was it okay to blow on it? Probably not. Trying not to look as if I was watching, I observed the Duchess fill the bowl of her soup spoon halfway and then hold it above the bowl, waiting for the contents to cool before spooning it into her mouth.

I copied her actions, not sure how I felt about eating anything the color of grass clippings. I was surprised by how tasty it was.

"Cream of green vegetable soup is one of my favorite soups," the Duchess said, waiting for her next spoonful to cool. "It contains leeks, peas, zucchini, celery, green beans, cilantro, parsley, kale, and spinach, which makes it not only tasty but also healthy. When Aaron was a child, he refused to eat it, claiming it looked like cream of grass and weed soup."

He wasn't wrong, but at this rate, it would take an hour to finish this course. When I got down to the bottom of the bowl, I did like the others, tipping it away from me to get the last little bit.

The second the Duke put down his spoon, like magic, someone appeared to clear the table. Jeeves returned to top up the wine while another person appeared with the second course. This one was a scoop of bright purple, orange, white, and green salad heaped in the center of a bib lettuce leaf. Food in this place was interesting as well as colorful. I could identify shredded carrots, beetroot, radishes, sweet potato, and broccoli, sprinkled with balsamic dressing. I reached for the salad fork and poked at the mound. Half of these vegetables were on my "avoid at all costs" list. I was surprised by the taste of them combined, no doubt due to Mrs. Brown's skills, but when the Duke set down his fork, I was happy to do the same. I'd eaten about half which I considered nothing short of a miracle.

Once again the server came in and cleared away the plates, this time, adding another utensil to those on the table, a spoon smaller than the demitasse one in the photograph had been.

Another person came out of the kitchen carrying a tray of tiny balls of sherbet in glass dishes.

"Are you enjoying dinner, Marissa?" the Duchess asked, placing a small amount of the tangy sorbet into her mouth.

"Very much. I've never tasted anything like it. My meals are usually far plainer fare."

The Duke chuckled. "Nothing wrong with fish and chips or a good burger. How did you find your first day here?"

"It's been great. You have a beautiful home, and my room is exquisite. I loved the garden and the flowers. The conservatory is like a visit to the Garden of Eden. Your granddaughters were precious, and you've all made me feel welcome."

I consumed my sorbet, enjoying the tartness of the lemon, while the others discussed the events planned for next week. At this rate, I would have to take another week's vacation when I got back home to recuperate.

Once more, Jeeves came into the room, this time with a bottle of red wine, which the Duke sampled and approved.

As the man filled our red wine glasses, the Duke explained that this was British wine from Surrey.

"I wasn't aware that Britain produced wines."

It was the perfect response because a lively conversation about wine accompanied the main course—roast beef, mashed potatoes, crisp green beans, and Yorkshire pudding. Everything was absolutely delicious.

By the time dessert, a scrumptious raspberry torte, was served, I knew everything there was to know about the British wine industry. Instead of tea, I elected to have a glass of ice wine to finish the meal as the conversation continued, this time dealing with tomorrow night's opera.

When the grandfather clock in the hall bonged ten, the Duke and Duchess stood and moved away from the table.

"As Marley knows," the Duchess said, "Friday is my hospital charities day. I understand you'll be playing tourist for part of the day. I hope you enjoy yourself. We're quite proud of our city. We'll meet in the lounge at six-thirty. *La Bohème* is one of my favorite operas. Puccini was a genius. Now, if you'll excuse us, Roderick and I will go to our rooms to watch the news. We like to keep abreast of things. Goodnight."

"I look forward to it. Goodnight." I'd never been to the opera. The closest I'd come was Gilbert and Sullivan's *HMS Pinafore* in Stratford, Ontario years ago. I just hoped I would be able to figure out what was going on. The opera was in Italian, and I didn't speak a word of it.

"You should probably call it a night," Marley stated. "I want to call Aaron before I turn in. Hopefully, a good night's sleep will help fight off jetlag. I'll meet you in the Breakfast Room at eight. I've asked Hazel to prepare two traditional English breakfasts."

"Which is?"

"Back bacon, sausage links, scrambled eggs because I know they're your favorites, grilled tomatoes, fried mushrooms, and fried bread."

"Fried bread? Do you mean toast?"

"It's a little like French toast without the batter. Hazel fries the slices in butter. You'll see. It's delicious. After breakfast, we'll do some sightseeing. I promise we'll have fun."

I hugged her and followed her out of the room to the hall. She went left and I went right to the elevator.

Within ten minutes, I was in bed, my laptop on my knees as I looked up the summary of Puccini's masterpiece. This time, there would be no surprises. My reading finished, I set the computer aside and snuggled into bed. I'd survived Day One. Bring on Day Two.

* * *

As expected, I awoke early Friday morning, surprisingly well-rested. I'd slept through the night for the first time in months—no nightmares about disasters to wake me. It was only six, but there was no way that I would be able to go back to sleep. Besides, this was my usual time to get up, and hadn't Marley said the sooner I got back into my usual routine, the better?

At home, I would pad into the kitchen, feed Frodo who would be demanding his breakfast, and then make myself a cup of coffee, which I might or might not get to finish while hot. Since that wouldn't be the case here, I got out of bed and walked over to the desk. I picked up the handset on the phone. There was no keypad. I was about to hang up when the phone rang at the other end of the line.

Someone picked up on the second ring. "Yes, Miss Kimble, what can I get you?"

I recognized Hazel's voice. Did she have a massive board down there that told her who was calling and from where?

"Yes ... Good morning. I hope I'm not bothering you. If it isn't too much trouble, could I have some coffee?"

"Of course. Right away. Would you like anything else?"

"Just sugar and cream, please. I'll be eating later with Marley."

"It'll be up shortly."

"Thank you." I wanted to ask how long shortly was—two minutes, ten—but she'd ended the call.

Shrugging, I went into the bathroom, answered nature's morning call, and then to the closet to get my robe and slippers.

Sitting at the desk, I opened the computer and called up my email. By the time I finished reading Bridget's response to my message, a knock at the door announced my coffee.

I opened the door. It was the girl I'd seen dusting in the formal room yesterday.

"Good morning. Just put it on the desk. Thanks ... I'm afraid I don't know your name."

The girl smiled shyly. "I'm Edith Brown."

"Megan's sister?" She nodded. "Thanks, Edith."

The girl, dressed in a black blouse and matching pants nodded. "Enjoy your day."

Herman's Hermits filled my head once more, and I hummed the song as I poured myself a cup of coffee that was every bit as good as it had been the previous day. After finishing the cup, I went into the bathroom, showered, and prepared to play *Tourist in London* for the day.

Not sure where Marley would be taking me, I wore my jeans, running shoes, and a navy tank top with a blue and white shirt over the top of it, well aware of my tendency to burn. Instead of my new tinted moisturizer, I used sunscreen. Since I had an hour to kill, I made my bed and then sat in the wingchair, and poured myself more coffee. I'd found a couple of books in the library that I was anxious to read.

At five to eight, I entered the Breakfast Room carrying the tray with the empty carafe, the cream and sugar, and my cup.

"You didn't have to do that," Marley said, taking them from me and setting them on the sideboard. "Someone would've brought them down after they made up your room."

"I was coming down anyway. I thought I would save someone a trip."

Marley laughed. "I'll bet you made your bed, too."

"Why wouldn't I? It's the first thing I do each day. People have enough to do keeping this place clean without having to look after me. I'm used to doing things for myself. I'm just visiting, remember?"

Marley shook her head. "I love you, you know that, don't you?"

"I do, and I love you, too."

Before she could say anything else, Edith came into the room with a fresh carafe of coffee. After she filled our cups, she placed the carafe between us. She went over to pick up the tray and carried it into the kitchen. Moments later, she was back with the two plates filled with breakfast.

"It smells delicious, thank you."

I was surprised by how hungry I was. After finishing off another cup of coffee, I made a trip to the water closet. By a quarter to nine, Marley and I were on our way to the Tower of London.

The traffic was heavier this morning than it had been yesterday, but Marley got us there early enough to see the Beefeater in full uniform, escorted to the imposing edifice by the guards. There, he used what she explained were called the King's Keys to unlock the door and officially open the building to tourists. She pointed out the spot in the courtyard where she'd backed into Aaron. We were careful not to jostle anyone. With my luck, instead of a lovestruck lord, it would be some rich potentate, and he'd sue me for everything I had.

The Tower of London originally constructed during the eleventh century served many purposes over the years. It had been a royal residence, as well as the royal mint, but its greatest claim to fame had been the times that it had served as a jail for political prisoners. Over the centuries, hundreds of people, both men and women had been kept there. Some were innocent, others not so much. I perused the long line of inmates, stopping when I came across a name I recognized, like William Wallace, the thirteenth-century Scottish leader and the main character played by Mel Gibson in the movie *Braveheart.*

Among this grim prison's inmates who were executed were three queens of England: Anne Boleyn, Catherine Howard, and Lady Jane Grey who ruled for only nine days. It wasn't a good century to be the queen.

Three other names caught my attention. Princess Elizabeth, who would go on to be Queen Elizabeth I, had spent a few months imprisoned there. Later on, so had Sir Walter Raleigh. As my index finger ran down the list, I found the name of the last political prisoner, Rudolph Hess, the deputy leader of the Nazi party. I shivered. Old history meeting the new. If they didn't keep them here, where *did* they keep political prisoners these days? Marley didn't know.

Like her, I found the legend about the ravens fascinating. Ravens were a common sight back in Canada, but to believe that if the birds left the Tower for whatever reason, the kingdom would fall, was as superstitious as you could get. Still, keeping a half-dozen on hand to show the tourists wasn't a bad idea. We met the official Yeoman Warder, or Raven Master, who tended to the birds caged in the Wakefield Tower. I might've felt sorry for the birds deprived of their freedom, but maybe that wasn't such a bad thing for them since the ravens in captivity had been known to live for more than forty years.

Our final stop on the Tower tour gave us a chance to see the crown jewels. Photography wasn't allowed and everything was under thick glass. The various tiaras, brooches, necklaces, earrings, and crowns boasted dazzling diamonds, rubies, emeralds, sapphires, gold, and silver. The Coronation Regalia and St. Edward's Crown, most recently used on May 6, 2023, for Charles III and Queen Camilla, were magnificent. Seeing them on television, even on a wide, flat screen, didn't do them justice.

By the time we finished our tour, it was time for lunch. Marley took me to one of her favorite pubs for fish and chips and a beer. While the brew wasn't what I was familiar with, it was delicious.

"I have a special surprise for the afternoon," Marley said, and the look on her face told me I might not agree. "I didn't want to mention it earlier because I didn't want you to argue with me about it."

Frowning, I set down my glass. "What is it?" I looked at her with the same wariness I would've given a tiger heading my way.

"I've arranged an afternoon at the spa. We'll get a massage followed by manicures and pedicures, have our hair done, and then have the cosmetician fix our makeup for tonight. I called ahead so they know the color of your dress. There's no better way to relax before an evening out."

I smiled. I could think of plenty of ways to relax, and this would not be one of them.

With all the stoicism and enthusiasm of someone being led to the gas chamber, I followed Marley down the street to the *Shangri-La Spa*.

"I really don't need all of this," I stated, trying to worm my way out of it. "You can go and I'll wander around. There's a bookstore over there I'd love to visit. It takes me little to no time to pull my hair into a chignon and slap on a fresh coat of moisturizer and lipstick."

She pleaded with her eyes. "Marissa, just this once, let me show you what you've been missing. Give it a try, please?"

What could I say to that?

I huffed out a breath. "Well, if it means that much to you..."

We entered the building through smoked glass doors.

"Miss Marley," the woman at the desk gushed even before the doors closed. "Ariana and Helga are waiting for you in Room Two."

"Thank you, Holly." She turned to me. "We leave our shoes here." She indicated the cubicles on the wall, some empty, others occupied, and removed her shoes.

I could see why. I'd never seen such thick, white carpets in my life. I slipped off my runners and put them in a cubicle next to the one she chose.

"This way."

With my feet sinking deeply into the lush carpet, I followed her to a room that turned out to be the fanciest locker room I'd ever seen.

"Do you come here often?"

She smiled. "Once every three weeks." She reached for one of the white velour robes on the shelf and handed it to me. "Get undressed. After the massage, we'll soak in a series of tubs filled with oiled water to soften the skin before showering. Then, we'll have our hands and feet done. After that, we'll have our hair done and lastly, we'll visit the cosmetician. In my line of work, I've come to understand how important the little things are, especially when meeting new people. I want you to enjoy this experience, so keep an open mind, okay?"

I nodded. How bad was this going to be?

Within seconds, my sister was as naked as the day she'd been born. Reluctantly, I undressed and put my clothing and my purse in a locker, securing it with a lock, and pocketing the key.

Marley led the way out of there into another room that smelled of vanilla and lavender. Two women in their thirties, wearing pink uniforms like the woman at the desk waited for us. Marley greeted them, introduced me, and then dropped the robe to lie on her stomach on the towel covered table. The woman draped another towel over her buttocks.

I swallowed. Was I ready to bare it all?

"Come on, Marissa, don't be shy. For heaven's sake. It's not the first time you've been naked in front of others. We all went skinny-dipping at the pond back home."

Yeah, but I'd been sixteen, and I'd known everyone there. This was not the same.

"Helga is one of the best masseuses here," she continued. "She'll get rid of all those kinks in no time."

"Easy for you to say," I grumbled. I liked my stiff muscles. We were old friends. What I didn't like was being touched by strangers, especially those who looked like they'd been on the Russian swim team in their teens. Wishing I were anywhere but here, I took off the robe and climbed onto the table, lying prone and longing for this to be over before it even started.

Helga rubbed oil onto my neck and shoulders and kneaded the muscles in my neck and back with the same enthusiasm as an angry baker who hated his job kneaded bread. By the time she'd finished, I felt as though I'd gone ten rounds in an MMA cage, but my shoulders were more relaxed.

We put on our robes once more and moved to the next room. There were a couple of people there Marley spoke to as she removed the robe once more. It took every ounce of courage I possessed to remove the robe. I wasn't used to being introduced to people when I was buck naked, but weirdly these people didn't seem to notice and chatted about the upcoming ball and the wedding as if sitting around in the altogether was an everyday occurrence.

The attendant came in and moved us on to the next pool. Slipping into the hot scented water was heaven. We moved from one hot tub to another. The scents changing from pool to pool.

Getting out of the last one, I moved with the group toward a massive wall of showers. I expected the water to be hot; after all, it was supposed to rinse off the last of the oils. Marley should've warned me.

"Jesus, Mary, Joseph," I screamed as the icy water from a dozen jets pummeled my body. My loud expletive must've tightened a hell of a lot more than pores, but no one commented, not even Marley.

If I never did that again, it would be too soon.

CHAPTER EIGHT

Not yet recovered from the icy shock to my heart and shivering, not in the least bit convinced that the subzero shower was the best way to seal my pores, I donned the robe once more and moved into the next chamber of horrors with the same exhilarating joy as I had the root canal I'd undergone six months ago. To be honest, the last time I'd had a pedicure in a salon had been twelve years ago, the day of the senior prom. Pedicures weren't necessary when you wore work boots every day. From the stunned look on the young Asian girl's face, I probably should've. My nails were clean and short, but let's just say the soles and heels were heavily callused.

Despite the fact that I'd spent the last hour in and out of tubs, she soaked my feet in what had to be a powerful skin softener. Once that task was accomplished, she trimmed my toenails, squaring off each one so that they were of uniform length.

So far the process hadn't been too bad, but then she pulled out what I suspected was a wallpaper-removing tool that looked like an industrial-strength cheese grater. With a grim look of determination on her face, she attacked the heels and then the soles of my feet while I struggled not to curse, swear, pull my ticklish feet out of her hands, or accidentally kick her in the face. That torture seemed to go on forever before the worst started. She poured lotion onto my feet and lower legs and began massaging. By the time she finished, I was seconds away from death by tickling. The final step was polishing. I watched in relief as she painted each toenail a gorgeous garnet to match my dress.

"Thank you so much," I gushed, not because my feet did look fantastic, but because I was grateful she'd finished.

She grinned. "Now, we'll do your hands."

Moving gingerly on slightly tender soles, I sat in the chair she indicated and extended both hands as instructed. From behind her, she pulled out a pot that looked suspiciously like a slow cooker and set it on the table in front of me before taking both of my hands and plunging them into the vat of hot paraffin wax.

This time, I smothered my curse. I'd given them enough to laugh at for months to come.

"This will soften your hands, leaving them smooth. It's the best I can do with so many calluses. I've never seen a lady..."

"I'm not a lady. I'm an electrician," I mumbled.

"Really? I've never met a female electrician before. Tell me about your job. It must be hard and dangerous." She pulled my hands out of the hot wax and wrapped my waxed paws in a towel.

"Staring down at the towel, I sighed and began telling her what my life was really like.

As I spoke, she unwrapped my hands and began removing the wax covering them. Ming asked questions about my life and Canada as she applied the gel nails, keeping them shorter than she probably did for most of the ladies here. By the time we'd finished talking, she'd turned my worker's hands into objects of beauty, my nails topped with the same gorgeous garnet polish that matched my feet. My hands looked lovely, but they wouldn't last a day on the job. That reality saddened me.

"You're definitely a miracle worker." I was impressed. As much as my job might be distasteful at times, hers had to be worse, especially when she had a client like me. I hoped they paid her well and tipped her extra for today. "Where to now?"

"Follow me. Remi will be ready for you."

I didn't know who Remi was, but I hoped the man would be as patient as Ming had been.

The woman escorted me into another room. Once more, I was the only occupant. There was a basin with a chair in front of it, another on wheels in front of a cloth-covered mirror, and a table covered in hair products. I sat at the basin as instructed. Within seconds, a young blond came in, introduced herself as Ava, and put my head back over the sink to wash and condition it. I was familiar with this process. Once my hair was clean, she led me to the chair in front of the mirror.

"You have beautiful hair. Remi will work wonders with it. He'll be in shortly."

Before I could thank her, she vanished through a door I hadn't noticed, and a man entered. Dressed in white from head to toe, Remi more closely resembled a surgeon than a hairstylist.

"Hello."

He didn't answer. Walking over to the chair, he cranked it up to make it easier for his impressive height. The man had to be six-foot-six. He spun the chair around and then reached for my hair, running his fingers through it before rubbing various strands together. He brushed it all away from my face and did whatever a hairdresser does to find the natural part.

He never said a word, before grabbing the hairdryer and drying the front and top of my head.

Suddenly, he was gone, leaving my hair sticking up every which way.

What the hell?

Before I could attempt to escape from the chair, he was back with a plastic bowl, a brush that looked a lot like the one I used to put barbecue sauce on ribs, and a box of aluminum foil. I swallowed.

"What's that for?"

"Quiet. I need silence to create."

Fine. He needed silence, but I wanted answers. Still, the scowl on his face kept me quiet.

With an efficiency I admired, he grabbed strands of hair, painted them with the liquid in the dish, and wrapped them in foil. He highlighted to his heart's content, before pulling over an old-fashioned hairdryer, the kind popular in the fifties and sixties, over my head, before disappearing once more.

Ava returned and handed me a glass of champagne—not the cheap stuff they served at midnight on New Year's Eve.

"Thank you." She vanished through the secret door once more.

The dryer stopped, and Ava was back.

"I'll just rinse the foils," she said, lowering the chair and leading me back to the basin.

Once I was back in the chair, my hair sopping wet once more, she left and Remi reappeared.

Without a word, he cranked me up again. He repeated his examination of my hair. He combed it and reached for the scissors on the table.

"I just had it cut."

He paid no attention to me and snipped away. Once he was done—and without a mirror how was I to know how much he'd cut—he set my hair on rollers the way I recall it had been done that night twelve years ago. Had I fallen through a hole in time? It certainly felt like it. Once more, he placed the egg-shaped hairdryer over my head and disappeared. Houdini couldn't have done any better.

The only good part was that Ava returned with another glass of champagne.

The champagne soothed my nerves, but I couldn't help feeling sorry for people who thought all of this was necessary for the sake of beauty.

The dryer stopped. He returned. Diligently, he removed each roller, using his fingers to keep the voluminous curls intact. Meticulously, he worked each tress, adding enough hairpins to secure it in place to have me avoiding magnets. He pulled the cloth off the mirror.

"It's done."

I could scarcely believe my eyes. He held up a large mirror to show me the back of my head. My stringy blond hair was a mass of loose, natural curls. Between the darker gold strands were ivory tresses that made my hair shine in a way it never had before. Without a word, he added enough hairspray to permanently cement the style in place.

"Wow. You're amazing."

He nodded his head and vanished once more.

"What about me? You said I was done," I called into the air, my voice bouncing off the walls. "Remi? Ava?"

I was about to try to get out of the chair and go searching for a familiar face when the door opened, and a woman entered, dragging a suitcase with her as large as my blue-patterned bag.

"Good afternoon, Miss Kimble. I'm Sally."

It was still afternoon? It seemed as if I'd been trapped in here for hours.

"Hello." I had to say something as she set about opening her bag to reveal pots, jars, palettes of eyeshadow, brushes, wands, tweezers, scissors, and God alone knew what else.

She turned the chair to face away from the mirror and got to work. Whereas Remi had been silent, Sally chattered like a magpie, explaining what she was doing as she worked. I couldn't imagine going to these lengths each day just to meet some perverted standard of beauty. It made sense for a movie star or a model but for everyone else, including me? No way. If I tried to do something like this each morning, not only would I be late for work, I would come off looking like the clown from *It*.

The cosmetician added another layer of paint to my lips and smiled. "You're very beautiful, Miss Kimble. Thank you for allowing me to make you shine." She handed me a mirror.

As if I had a choice. Mirror, mirror in my hand, who's the fairest in the land?

When she turned me to face the larger mirror, I gasped.

"That's me?"

If I were to meet myself on the street, I would never recognize myself. The woman staring back at me was posh and sophisticated, her complexion smooth and even. The blue-gray eye shadow, eyeliner, and black mascara gave size and depth to my sapphire eyes. The creamy peach foundation hid the marks and freckles on my face, while the pink blush highlighted cheekbones I didn't even know I had. Sally had used a deep garnet lipliner and then a garnet lip paint with a coat of clear lip shine on top to make my lips fuller and more symmetrical. I was ... I was ... beautiful and hot ... and fake.

Swallowing my disappointment that the lovely woman staring back at me in the mirror wasn't me and never would be, I smiled, blinking rapidly to avoid the possibility of tears.

"Thank you so much."

Sally smiled. "It seems quite shocking to you, doesn't it? It usually does when a woman who's never realized her own potential sees herself for the first time."

"I ... I ... don't usually have time for stuff like this."

"Every woman has the time. She just needs to want to take it. I quite like you. You remind me of why I wanted to do this job in the first place, and that's refreshing. Cosmetics can't make a woman beautiful. They simply enhance what's there, but true beauty radiates from inside and shines through. Have fun tonight."

I nodded, but before I could say anything else, Marley came into the room. Her own hair had been styled, and since she always wore makeup of some sort, there had been no dramatic change.

"Marissa." She squealed as if someone had stuck her with a pin. "You're even more beautiful than I knew you would be. You're going to knock 'em dead," Marley said. "I can't wait for Mom and Dad to see you. I knew this afternoon would be worth it, but the staff exceeded my expectations. Now, let's get going. It's after five. We're later than I expected. We have to be ready and downstairs by six-thirty."

"Aye-aye, Captain." I resorted to the name Mom gave Dad when he was bossing everyone around. "All I have to do is put on my dress. That won't take much time."

She hustled me out of the room and back to the locker room. Big Ben bonged six when we pulled into the driveway of Renfield House.

A man, another one I didn't know, rushed down the steps even before the car came to a stop.

"Thanks, Phillips," Marley said, handing the car keys to the man. "I won't be needing the car again this week." She turned to me. "Since the

Duchess and Mom will be with us tomorrow morning, we'll take the Bentley."

Hurrying me to the elevator, I'd just entered my room when Edith arrived to help me dress. I was about to send her away when I realized that I would need help if I didn't want to make a mess of my hair. I'd tried on the dress, but I hadn't been able to zip it up all the way by myself. She held the dress while I stepped into it—I would've probably tried to pull it over my head and ruined my hair—and zipped up the back while I slid my feet into the matching high-heeled shoes.

I stood in front of the mirror. I stared at the gorgeous reflection. I didn't know that stranger looking back at me, but damn if I didn't want to be her.

"You look smashing, Miss Kimble. That color becomes you."

"Thank you." I reached for my gold hoops.

The door opened, and Marley came in.

She wore a seafoam, knee-length sleeveless dress with a square neckline that set off the gorgeous aquamarine necklace fastened at her neck.

I smiled, probably for the first time since this morning.

"You look stunning. I love the necklace. It's perfect for the dress. Are those diamonds?"

Marley shook her head. "Swarovski crystals. I bought the set when I was in Vienna last month. I bought these for you to wear tonight as well."

She handed me a small box.

"I told you I was giving you something more practical than a baby horse."

I opened the box. Inside was a pair of garnet and crystal chandelier earrings with a matching necklace that would enhance my outfit perfectly.

"Marley, they're gorgeous."

"Garnets are your birthstones since your birthday is in January, and I wanted to give you at least one thing that you would be willing to use again."

I pulled her into my arms, careful not to mess up her makeup or hair.

"Don't for a minute think I don't love all of the things you've given me. This is a once in a lifetime opportunity, one I'll cherish long after I'm back on my hands and knees running wire. I promise I will wear these again." The only jewelry I ever wore were earrings, my one concession to the girly girl inside me.

I went over to the mirror and put on the earrings, which were the perfect size and length. Was that posh woman really Marissa Kimble, an electrician from Brockton, Ontario? It didn't seem possible and yet, it was. I thought about a souvenir mug that I'd picked up last year when I'd visited the *Mark Twain House and Museum* in Hartford Connecticut while attending an electricians' conference. It said: *Clothes make the man,* or in my case, the woman. *Naked people have little or no influence in society.* Dressed like this, I could probably influence anyone I liked—dukes, duchesses, lords, ladies, even Zak.

"The Duke and Duchess are in the library with Mom, Dad, and Aaron. I can't wait for them to see you."

What would they see? Me or the painted doll I'd become?

I slipped my arms into the jacket that matched my dress, allowing Edith to settle my hair over it, grabbed my clutch purse, and followed Marley out of the room, waiting as she went into her own room to get the cape that went with her dress. As soon as she joined me once more, I pressed the call button for the elevator.

The doors swished open. Marley stepped out and I followed her.

The momentary silence was unexpected before Mom and Dad started talking all at once.

"Darling, I've never seen you look lovelier," Mom said, stepping over to hug me.

Dad reached for me when she released me. "I always knew you were a diamond in the rough. You look great."

Had I really looked that bad before? No wonder Zak had chosen Karen over me.

"Thanks, but it's all smoke and mirrors. A little magic on the part of gifted people. I'll be back to the old me before you know it."

Mom frowned but didn't say anything.

"Rissa," Marley said, taking my arm and leading me over to the tall, dark-haired man standing next to the Duke and Duchess. The strands of silver at the temples didn't detract from his good looks. "This is Aaron, the love of my life."

Aaron bent to kiss his fiancée's cheek. "Darling, you're more beautiful than ever." He turned his megawatt smile on me and held out his hand. "Marissa, it's a pleasure to meet you. Marley sang your praises. I can see that she didn't exaggerate in the least."

"Thank you. It's nice to meet you, too. I've heard a lot about you, all of it good."

"I'll add my compliments, Marissa," the Duke said, "but I suggest we get going. The curtain goes up at seven-fifteen, and I hate to have to step over people to be seated."

The Duchess stepped beside him and slipped her arm into his. She smiled at me and winked.

"You'll have a wonderful time tonight."

Why did I suddenly have that *other shoe is about to fall* feeling?

I glanced at Marley, but she was engrossed in Aaron, and when I looked at Mom and Dad, both bore that *cat has swallowed the canary* look.

This couldn't be good.

* * *

Not used to being the center of attraction, I was grateful to finally arrive at the theater and give everyone something else to fuss about. The Bentley rolled to a stop in front of *the English National Opera House* in Covent Garden, and Austin came around to open the door. Aaron got out first, then turned to help Marley and Mom. The Duke exited next and then the Duchess. Finally, it was my turn since Dad had sat up front with Austin. He'd never been able to sit in the back seat of any vehicle.

I had no warning as desire, as strong and primitive as the need to breathe to survive, grabbed me the second I stepped onto the sidewalk and saw who waited there.

"Zak," Aaron said loudly, "I'm so glad you were able to make it. I thought the problem with Briar Rose would keep you away."

While I wanted to run and hide, there was no place to go, not if I wanted to maintain what little dignity I had. I turned to look accusingly at Marley, but she was facing away, adjusting Dad's bowtie. Had she known Zak would be here? Was that why I'd been part of a dog and pony show this afternoon?

"Actually, the mare settled in well once she saw Crimson. They were stablemates at Cedar Glen, so it was like meeting an old friend. I don't anticipate any problems."

"Good to hear. Jacob's hoping Crimson will do well at the race on Sunday."

"He should. He's in top form. Even if he doesn't win, he'll place, and that's not bad for a first outing."

I shuffled over slightly to stay hidden behind the Duke. The sound of Zak's voice filled me with longing. I glanced between the Duke and Duchess to get a better look at the man I'd loved and had lost.

Like the other men, he was dressed formally, wearing a dark gray suit with a white shirt and a black and gray striped tie. His chestnut hair was still cut short, but it was sprinkled with silver. He'd grown a beard since our time together, and it suited him. In this light and from this distance, I couldn't read the expression in his eyes, but he seemed relaxed, while I was on pins and needles.

Aaron led Zak over to the spot where we stood. Austin pulled away from the curb, leaving me feeling exposed.

"Zak, I know you met my father yesterday at Knightsbridge, but allow me to present my mother Elise Sykes, the Duchess of Habersham."

"Your Grace." He executed a perfect head bow and smiled. "It's a pleasure to meet you."

"Dr. Mitchum. I've heard a lot about you, young man. My son is well-pleased with your services."

"Thank you."

"You know your stuff, Dr. Mitchum." The Duke stepped forward and extended his hand. "Leon's implemented your suggestions concerning Caesar. Putting him out to pasture with the other horses has improved his disposition."

Zak reached for the Duke's proffered hand. "Horses, like people, are sensitive to their environments. Sometimes all a high-strung animal needs are the right companions."

I stood statue-still. There was no way Zak couldn't see me and yet he showed no sign of interest or recognition. What had I expected? After Sally's magic, I hadn't recognized myself either.

"You know my future in-laws, Mitchell and Moira Kimble," Aaron continued.

"Mitchell, Moira." Zak shook both of their hands. "It's been a while. How's that prize bull doing?"

Dad chuckled. "Since you gave him that tonic, he's back to his old virile self."

Mom smiled at him as if she'd known he would be there. Maybe she had. No one seemed as surprised as they should be.

"You're looking well," Mom said. "How's your father? Is the gout still bothering him?"

"It's not as bad since he agreed to change his diet and take his pills, but Mom still has to watch him like a hawk. The man's addicted to salt. How have you enjoyed your European vacation?"

"We're having the time of our lives, and this wedding and having both my girls here..."

The Duke and Duchess stepped away from me. Zak's head swiveled. I knew the moment he realized it was me. His jaw dropped hard enough to shatter on the pavement.

"Marissa?" He choked out my name, his eyes bulging as he raked me from head to toe. The shock and awe in his voice were unsettling. The scene would've been funny if it hadn't been so tragic and brought back the memory of his similar reaction five years ago. His eyes widened, not in confusion like back then, but in admiration. He shook his head, raising his hands, palms open wide. "You look ... you look ... incredible. I can hardly believe it's you."

Had I really changed that much? I'd always believed that you dressed to reflect the person you wanted to be, and this wasn't who I was. Under the paint and fancy gown, I was still the tomboy who wanted to be an electrician, the girl who wanted to play football. Why could no one see that? I buried my pain under the Ice Queen veneer I'd worn five years ago.

"Different? Yes, but it has been five years. We all change. You're looking well." I managed to say, my voice composed, even though each heated glance he gave me was cutting away at my courage and aplomb.

"You look fantastic." He stared at me, the emotions in his eyes discomfiting.

"Nothing an expensive dress and a day at the spa can't accomplish." The ice in my voice could've turned the Sahara Desert into the Tundra.

The Duke cleared his throat. "Shall we go inside? We seem to be attracting more attention than I'd like."

I was suddenly aware of all the people with cameras loitering in front of the building.

The Duke took the Duchess's arm, Dad reached for Mom's, Aaron laced his fingers with Marley's and tucked their joined hands into the crook of his arm, leaving me with Zak. He offered me his arm. I looked at it as if it was a rattlesnake, but aware of the paparazzi, I slipped my arm into the crook of his, and without a word, let him lead me inside. The heat emanating from his body almost overwhelmed me with memories of times long past, times before Karen, times before his infidelity had ruined everything.

Once we were inside, away from the prying eyes of the yellow press, I tried to step away from him. He put his hand on my arm to keep me in place.

"You misunderstood my reaction. It isn't your clothes or makeup ... It's you, just you. You've always been beautiful to me, Rissa. It's been so long. I knew I would be seeing you tonight ... I just never expected it would hit me so hard. I've missed you. We need to talk—"

I stepped away from him, forcing him to let go of me. I straightened my jacket, fighting for my earlier composure. "I can't imagine what we have to discuss," I straightened. "Marley told me you would be at the wedding. I agreed to be pleasant and polite, and I will be, but that's all I'll be ... for her sake. The past is dead and buried. Let's leave it there. Nothing good comes from beating a dead horse. And as for missing me, I find that hard to believe."

His eyes filled with confusion.

Before he could speak, I stepped over to stand next to my parents until the usher led us to our seats. As luck would have it, he was seated on my left, with the Duchess on my right, in the center of the front row of the mezzanine, no doubt the best seats in the entire theater. The building was incredible, a marvel of an earlier time and place. Tourist that I was, I snapped several pictures, making sure he wasn't in any of them, certain none of them would turn out with the way my hand was trembling.

The opera was exquisite, but if you asked me a single detail about it, I couldn't give you one. I kept my eyes fixed on the stage but saw nothing, consumed by the sensation of his eyes on me. At the first intermission, I excused myself to go to the ladies' room. Marley followed me.

"I swear I didn't know Aaron had given him a ticket," she whispered into my ear as soon as we stepped into the room.

I shrugged and headed for an empty stall. "It's okay. I would've met him sooner or later. What we had is over and done. It's finished. I told you that once I saw him, I'd be able to put everything into perspective."

Closing the door, I forced myself to deal with the matter at hand. I would get through this night one way or the other.

When I came out of the stall, I washed my hands, then added a coat of gloss to my painted lips.

"You're sure you're okay? I was afraid you'd be upset," Marley washed her hands and dried them on the cloth hand towels, dropping the used one into the basket.

"I'm fine," I lied. "What we had would never have worked. I see that now. I'm looking forward to seeing Ken at the after-show supper. It's all good. Now, let's go back and enjoy the rest of the opera."

Marley frowned, the doubt in her eyes easy to recognize. "Are you sure?"

"Absolutely."

But it wasn't good. I wasn't fine, and I knew it.

CHAPTER NINE

During the second half of the opera, I forced myself to focus on the presentation, convincing myself that the shock of seeing Zak had worn off, and I was, as I'd assured my sister, fine. Every now and then, I glanced at him out of the corner of my eye, only to find him looking at me, with hunger on his face and sorrow in his eyes.

After the second curtain call, he reached for my arm. "Please, Marissa, just give me a chance to talk to you alone. You may not want to talk about the past, but there's too much left unsaid between us to ignore. Don't I deserve closure?"

He didn't deserve a damn thing, but he looked so miserable that I nodded. If anyone deserved closure, it was me.

"Fine. We'll talk at Knightsbridge. It shouldn't be too hard to find the time since we'll be staying in the same house."

His brow furrowed, and his eyes narrowed. The muscle in his jaw jumped. I thought he might argue the point, but then he sighed and nodded.

"Fine, Knightsbridge it is, but we will talk, Marissa. Count on it. You can't leave without giving me an explanation. Not this time." He turned to Aaron. "I have my own car, so I'll meet you at the restaurant."

Aaron had been standing next to me and could hardly have failed to notice the tension between us, but he simply nodded. "We'll see you there."

I was about to get into the car when Zak reached out to me and took my hand. His gaze fastened on my eyes, and he raised my hand to his lips. He turned my hand palm up and his lips brushed the tender skin there, sending shivers and coils of heat warring through me.

"We aren't finished, Marissa, not by a long shot. It was wonderful to see you again. I look forward to more time with you." With that, he turned and left.

Seeing me again? The damn fool hadn't even recognized me, and as far as being finished went, we were way past finished.

"Such a nice young man," the Duchess said, her eyes twinkling, a tiny smile on her lips. "He's quite fond of you, and yet, you seem intent on pushing him away. I take it you have unresolved issues?"

I shrugged. It was probably a major breach of etiquette to tell her to mind her own business.

"As far as I'm concerned, Your Grace, what Zak and I had ended a long time ago."

The Duchess pursed her lips and shook her head. "Young people. Have you heard the expression, don't throw the baby out with the bathwater?"

I chuckled. "Of course, but it's never made much sense to me."

"That's because you don't understand it. Years ago, bathing was a time-consuming and difficult process undertaken infrequently. The tub would be filled with hot water, and the head of the household would bathe first, then the eldest son, and so on according to age and status. By the time the youngest got into the bath, the water was usually quite cloudy and dirty. One had to look carefully to make sure no one was left in the tub. Today, it applies to anything that is set aside without careful investigation. Relationships fall into that category. Marissa, that young man cares for you. I can see from your eyes that he did something that hurt you deeply, but before you throw love away, remember things are not always as they seem."

"Your Grace, in this case, there was no mistake." I swiped at my eye, surprised to feel the tear there, hoping the makeup was waterproof, and I wasn't about to resemble a raccoon. "I wish it had been."

It was almost eleven when we entered the restaurant. Zak hadn't arrived yet, so I relaxed.

This supper club was one of London's finest. The Maître D escorted us to a table near the dance floor. When I saw Ken waiting, I was ready to weep for joy—not because he was there, but because I would have a buffer between myself and Zak. As I'd expected, he did a double take when I walked over to the table, with Aaron and Marley leading the way, but he recognized me before his mouth split into a wide, appreciative smile.

"Marissa Kimble, you are absolutely gorgeous. There isn't an electrician in the world who could shine brighter than you do right now. Of course, you're always beautiful, even in short shorts the way you were when I saw you last." He winked. "I don't know what you've done to yourself, but I like it, not that I don't like you the way you usually look."

It was what I needed to hear, someone who could still see the old me in this new me. Someone who could appreciate that this wasn't the way I wanted to be.

"You don't look so bad yourself." He wore a dark suit, gray shirt, and a black and gray striped tie. "As to what I did, well, that's Marley's doing. She hired an army of experts to turn this pig's ear into a silk purse."

His smile widened as he stood and pulled me into a hug. "There's that sarcastic sense of humor I've missed. You may be any number of wild and wonderful things, but you know damn well that you're not, and never were, a pig's ear. If anything, staying with the pork analogy, you're bacon, and I love bacon." He kissed me on the cheek, just below the ear. Tiny shivers danced along my skin. "I've never understood why you chose to stay in the background." He turned to Marley. "Of course, you, my lady, are as enchanting and gracious as ever."

"And you're so full of it that those eyes of yours should be brown instead of green." She laughed. "You haven't changed."

He stiffened, his eyes clouding with emotion. "But I have. I'm simply stating the truth. You and Marissa are the most beautiful women here. Thanks again for asking us to join you tonight and tomorrow. I'm looking forward to it."

Us?

The Duchess stepped forward her eyes filled with curiosity. "Marley, I don't believe I've met this young man."

"You haven't. Ken Atchison, allow me to introduce the Duchess of Habersham, my future mother-in-law, and this is the Duke, and my fiancé, Aaron Sykes, Lord Broadmere. Your Grace," Marley used the title to address the Duchess since we were in public. "Ken is an old, dear friend from Cedar Lake. He, Marissa, and his twin sister, Karen share the same birthday. They were inseparable as kids. When I discovered they were in London, I invited them to join us. I thought it would be nice for Marissa to have people around that she knew."

"Very commendable, my dear," the Duchess said before holding out her hand to Ken who was just releasing the Duke's.

"It's a pleasure to meet you, Ken. How are you enjoying London?"

"It's a lot to take in during the short period of time I have. I'm based in Newcastle. This is just the second time that I've been here. I'm hoping to see more of it, but right now, its main attraction is right beside me." He smiled at me.

There was no mistaking the desire in his eyes. I hadn't been wrong about Ken's intent and interest back in May. He was definitely flirting with me. How did I feel about him? I'd enjoyed our time together that night, but was it enough? And there was still the issue of that night five years ago hanging between us.

The Duchess smiled. "Well said, young man, well said."

My parents joined us since my mother had stopped in the water closet to freshen up. As expected, Mom and Dad treated Ken like a family member the way they always had. I suppose since we'd done so much together as children, it was to be expected. After all, I'd always referred to his parents as Aunt Sarah and Uncle Joel. When it came right down to it, he was the big brother I'd never realized I had. Siblings might fight like cats and dogs when they were young, but they usually grew closer with age. That had certainly been true with Marley and me, why not with Ken and Karen? Of course, I would need to forgive her first, and that wasn't likely to happen during this lifetime.

I moved aside to let my mother get closer to him.

"Ken, you look well. Much better than the last time I saw you in Calgary after the accident. How's your sister? Is she enjoying England?"

I frowned. Ken had spoken about his accident and had implied it had changed him, but I'd assumed it had been because he'd been scared. How serious had it been? I'd noticed a slight limp when we were dancing. I'd simply assumed he'd broken his leg. Had it been more than that? Mom hadn't said a word, but Ken and Zak had been unmentionable subjects. I would make a point of asking her about it tomorrow.

Ken grinned. "I'm a different man than I was then, Aunt Moira. Facing Death and spitting in his eye makes you think twice about a second encounter, especially when he leaves behind a permanent reminder. As for Karen, she loves this country, but you can talk to her about it. She had a call to make, but she should be right back."

A permanent reminder? Scars and maybe that limp? The rest of what he said filtered into my brain. Karen was here? Now? Would she blurt out the truth about that night? Would she laugh and make a sarcastic comment about the painted doll in glad rags? I might look like a different person, but inside I was still the same terrified and humiliated Marissa Kimble. I wasn't ready to face the enemy and do battle. Could I plead a headache and get a cab home? Knowing I couldn't, I sat on the chair next to Ken, the Duchess opting for the chair beside me.

Ken turned to me. "I took it upon myself to order you your favorite drink. Here it comes now."

The tuxedoed waiter set a beer glass in front of Ken, a tall glass of something clear and fizzy at the place on his right, and a deep pink cocktail coupe in front of me.

"As you ordered, sir. It's a Match. The bartender had to look it up. It's the first time he has."

The man stood there waiting. I reached for the glass and sipped, the tart strawberry taste as pleasant as I recalled.

"It's delicious, thank him, please."

The waiter nodded and smiled. He turned to the rest of the party. "Can I get you a beverage?"

"That looks interesting," Marley said, her head cocked to the right toward Mom.

"Yes," Mom agreed. "Rissa, when did you have one of those?"

"When Ken came to see me in Brockton a few weeks ago. We had dinner together, and even did a little dancing," I admitted, smiling at him. "Thank you. It's so nice that you remembered." Although right now I'd be happier with a bottle of whiskey, Frodo, and the confines of my room back in Brockton.

"How could I forget?" He spoke softly but not quietly enough not to be overheard. "It was one of the best nights I've had in a very long time."

Marley's eyebrows rose at Ken's words. She glanced at me, her gaze warning me that I would have some explaining to do later.

I looked down at the black cloth on the table, wishing the evening was over.

Mom and Marley ordered the same drink I had, while the Duchess asked for a champagne cocktail, and the Duke, Dad, and Aaron each ordered a scotch neat. I'd discovered that ice in drinks wasn't a popular thing here. I stared at the two empty seats beside Ken. Zak would have to sit next to Karen. How fitting.

My stomach somersaulted when I saw him enter the room. Even from this distance, I could see the scowl settle on his face. By the time he reached the table, he'd controlled his features and smiled broadly, even if the smile didn't reach his eyes.

"Ken Atchison. I didn't know you were in London," Zak said. "How have you been? I heard about your leg. Your recovery was nothing short of miraculous. I meant to give you a call, but I switched my work, and you took a job with that green energy company."

Ken must've downplayed the severity of his injuries. He'd joked about facing death, but I thought he'd simply been exaggerating, something he'd done in the past.

He chuckled. "I'm just glad I did recover. As for the job, I needed a change. You're looking well. I heard you'd taken over the large animal side of the clinic."

"Yes." Zak stuck out his hand and shook Ken's. "The hours are a little more convoluted, but I'd had enough of cats and pampered pooches to last me a lifetime."

"As I live and breathe. Zakary Mitchum. You are the last person I ever expected to see here."

The woman dressed in a black satin pantsuit propelled herself into Zak's arms.

He stood there as if carved from stone. His eyes widened and his jaw tightened, not the look I would've expected on the face of a man meeting his former lover.

Ken glanced at me, then at Zak, then at Karen, and back to me once more. Fate was one cruel mistress. She'd brought the four characters of a five-year-old tragedy together again. Was she expecting an encore? She wouldn't get it from me.

I looked away, right into the Duchess's gaze. Her eyes narrowed, her lips pursed, and she nodded slightly in a *now, I understand* motion.

I leaned back, not ready to be included in this farce just yet. Sensing eyes on me, I looked over to see Mom's concerned ones. Once more, I took a drink.

"Karen. It's been a while." Zak, his face flushed, disentangled himself from her.

Karen frowned slightly. "What are you doing here? Don't tell me you've returned to the Motherland, too?"

Zak shook his head. "I look after Lord Broadmere's horses back in Cedar Glen, his stud farm near Cedar Lake. He offered me a ticket to the opera tonight. I was anxious to see Marissa again. Seeing you and Ken is a ... pleasant surprise."

His comment lacked sincerity and from the slight pout on Karen's face, she knew it.

"Speaking of Marissa, where is she?" Karen, as bold and brash as ever, grabbed Zak's hand and led him around the table, sitting down next to her brother, leaving Zak no choice but to sit next to her. Ken put his arm around my shoulder and pulled me forward so that she could see me. "She's right here. You know Rissa. She likes to try and blend into the background, but not tonight."

Just this once, why couldn't the earth open up and swallow me whole?

Zak frowned but quickly hid his emotions. He didn't like Ken touching me? Too bad.

Karen's eyes grew the size of saucers. "Marissa? My God. I didn't even recognize you. What ... how ... you look ... fabulous, absolutely fabulous. You always had that down-home freshness about you, but this suave sophisticated look is gorgeous. I can't believe it's you. I was hoping to see you while you're in London."

I certainly hadn't been hoping to see her. In fact, I'd hoped to avoid her altogether both in the city and at the wedding. It was always easier to make yourself scarce in a crowd. Marley hadn't mentioned inviting her to tomorrow night's ball. Was there any way I could avoid attending? Probably not. Short of dying, there was no excuse I could come up with that Mom would buy.

Karen jumped up from her chair, rushed around behind Ken, and pulled me up into a hug.

"Oh, God. It's been so long." She pulled away, her eyes moist. "I'm so happy to see you ... I think I'm going to cry." She blinked rapidly.

What the hell? Who was this woman, and where was the real Karen Atchison? I returned the hug awkwardly.

"I'm just as surprised as you are," I said, well aware of the curious glances the four of us were getting from the other six in our party not to mention the other restaurant patrons, some of which were no doubt the paparazzi. "It's been a long time. Ken mentioned you were working here when he came to see me before leaving for Newcastle. You're looking well."

Actually, she looked fantastic. Her hair had been colored to look more blond than it had the last time I'd seen her and had been cut short. Instead of the heavy, dark eye makeup I recalled, she wore tan eyeshadow and mascara that brought out the green in her eyes, a light natural looking foundation, a touch of blush, and coral lipstick. As well, she'd gone from being the emaciated, weight-conscious girl I recalled to one with just the right amount of curves.

The Duchess smiled at me, my cue to introduce Karen.

"Your Grace, allow me to introduce Karen Atchison, Ken's twin sister. This lovely lady is the Duchess of Habersham."

Karen executed a head bow. "Your Grace, it's a pleasure to meet you."

The Duchess smiled. "I can see the resemblance between you and your brother, but you and Marissa look alike, too. Are you related?"

Karen nodded. "Distant cousins, but people used to joke about the Atchison triplets when we were younger. Since we shared everything including a birthday—Marissa is older than Ken by about thirty minutes and I arrived twenty minutes after that—we competed for everything as kids." She chuckled. "I'm grateful for this opportunity to see her again. It's nice having my brother and almost sister close again, even if it is only for a few days."

She released my hand, and I dropped into my chair, fighting to keep the shock off my face. Almost sister? I had to be hallucinating.

She moved back to her chair, stopping behind mine on the way.

"Marissa, I want to hear all about your life. Ken mentioned you owned your own business. That's wonderful. It was your dream, right?"

"It was ... it is." It might not have been the only dream, but no one could have everything in life.

She wanted to hear about *my* life? Why? So she could somehow ruin it? The butter wouldn't melt in her mouth look she was giving didn't fool me. People might think of her as kind and sweet, an angel of mercy, but I knew the truth. She was cruel, cold, and manipulative. She was up to something. She was always up to something. Who was she performing for? Zak? The Duke and Duchess? Whoever it was, she deserved an Oscar for faked sincerity.

Ken smiled, reached for my hand, and brought it to his lips. What was he doing? Everyone would get the wrong message ... that is if I knew what the right one was. Knowing I couldn't pull my hand away since that would just add to the confusion, I grabbed my drink with my free one and took a sip, praying I wouldn't choke on it.

"Marley invited us to the wedding a few weeks ago, but she called earlier this week and asked if we wanted to attend the masquerade ball tomorrow night, and then mentioned that you were all coming for a meal after the opera if we wanted to join you," Ken explained, turning to gaze at me with puppy dog eyes. "I knew you'd be here, but I didn't mention it to Karen since I wanted to surprise her. But seeing Zak is an unexpected pleasure. The four of us were really close."

And so were the Four Horsemen of the Apocalypse. Conquest, War, Famine, and Death. Karen was Conquest, and I was Death, or at least my heart had died. It was a toss-up as to which one of the remaining two was Zak.

Why was he explaining all this to me?

The waiter returned with the other drink orders. Zak ordered a highball. Once it was delivered, Aaron stood and thanked everyone for being here and proposed a toast to his fiancée and then another to the Canadians who'd joined in this momentous occasion. The servers arrived with the first course of the pre-ordered dinner, a cold plate featuring several seafood selections. Luckily, the appropriate cutlery arrived with the plate, too. I ate but the food could've been sawdust. I picked at the second course, not interested in food.

They'd just taken away the dessert plates when the band came onto the small stage and began to play. Aaron reached for Marley's hand.

"Don't be shy. Get up and dance. The band is playing this set at my request."

I recognized the intro and knew the song before the singer sang the first line, "Unchained Melody," by the Righteous Brothers.

Ken stood. "Come on, Marissa. I may not be the world's best dancer, but I manage a mean slow dance as you recall. I've waited a long time to hold you in my arms again."

Zak's gaze was on us as we left the table. When I turned into Ken's arms, I saw him lean over and whisper something to Karen. A few minutes later, the two of them joined us on the dance floor.

When the music changed to an upbeat tune, we returned to the table with the others and sipped our drinks. I danced with Aaron, the Duke, and my father before Zak asked me to. I couldn't very well refuse. This time, the singer was a woman, and she sang Taylor Swift's "Lover." Ken danced with his sister, but I could feel him watching Zak and me.

At first, I held myself stiffly in Zak's arms, but as the lyrics and music filled me, I relaxed. He didn't speak, but held me close, his heart pounding under my ear as memories of the good times we'd had before it had all gone so wrong flooded me. When the song ended, I excused myself to go to the water closet. I needed to be alone.

Glancing into the mirror, I saw the pain and regret in the painted doll's eyes. I still loved him.

I'd never stopped, and yet I cared for Ken in a way I never had before. I'd gone from being the angry victim to being caught in a different kind of emotional web. Forcing my conflicted feelings deep inside, for the first time ever I found myself wishing I was indeed the Ice Queen. I returned to the table, settled next to Ken, and reached for the new pink drink in front of me.

By the time the evening wrapped up, and we headed out to the car, I had a splitting headache. The knots Helga had unraveled in my neck and shoulders were back with a vengeance. I sighed. It was well after two, and we had to be at Madame Denise's at ten in the morning for the fittings, something I knew I wouldn't enjoy. All I could do was hope the process wouldn't take too long. I needed time to think before I faced Ken and Karen again. Would Zak be there, too? I didn't know and damn well wasn't going to ask. He'd left a short while earlier and had offered to drop Karen off. Maybe those two would have a little early morning delight to celebrate their reunion. Jealousy clawed at my gut.

Aaron offered to drop Ken at his hotel, but he declined.

"It's only a couple of blocks away. I'm not used to eating this late in the day. I'm a little stiff, but the walk will do me good."

Ken escorted me to the car, and before I could protest, pulled me into his arms for a goodnight kiss. My heart as sore as it was, I poured everything I had into reciprocating, and while it was nice to be wanted, there were no sparks. I ended it as quickly as I could, not missing the confusion in Ken's eyes. What had he felt? Had he had the same flat feeling I'd gotten? Had it felt like kissing your sibling as they said?

Not wanting to deal with that now, I smiled. "I'll see you tonight." Then, as quickly as I could, I escaped into the car.

The ride home was shorter than it had been when we'd gone to the opera, thanks to the deserted streets. As soon as we got into the house, I excused myself, thanked Aaron for the lovely evening, and rather than wait for the elevator, I removed my shoes and climbed the stairs to the third floor. I needed an analgesic, but more than that, I needed to be alone with my jumbled thoughts and emotions.

Seeing Zak had not made the pain of his betrayal any less. I'd lied to my sister. What it had done was rip the bandage off the old festering wound, exposing it anew, and it was hemorrhaging.

I undressed and hung my garnet dress in the closet. Cinderella was home from the ball. The coach hadn't turned into a pumpkin, but that didn't mean anything. It was time to get rid of my disguise. Painstakingly, I removed pin after pin from my hair, eventually managing to brush it out. Then, I used cold cream to remove the cosmetics on my face, followed by bar soap and a facecloth. The reflection in the mirror was a pale shadow of the one I'd seen earlier, the one with stars of wonder in her eyes. This woman's eyes were sad and filled with pain. The dark circles under them weren't caused by mascara, but by a broken heart, one that had started bleeding anew. How would I ever be able to face anyone and hide this sorrow from them?

Too tired to think about anything any longer, I crawled into bed, hoping for a few hours of sleep. I lay on my left side, closed my eyes, and took several deep breaths the way I always did as I waited for the sandman. He didn't come.

I tossed and turned, trying to get comfortable. It didn't work. I tried counting backward, counting sheep, counting my heartbeats, but sleep eluded me. Eventually, I must've drifted off.

Less than seven hours later, I was awake again after a night wrought in hell, filled with nightmares and tears. I dragged myself out of bed at nine. As usual, only wisps of the dreams remained in which Ken and Zak had battled over who had the best excuse for what had happened that night five years ago, Karen laughing in the background, and the Duchess repeating that things weren't always what they seemed.

I rubbed at my temples and the grit in my eyes. The remnants of last night's headache persisted. Hangover or lack of sleep? I didn't know. If I could, I would stay in bed until it was time to return to Brockton, but that was impossible. I took two analgesic tablets, showered, and pulled my hair into a loose ponytail at the nape, wondering briefly if I should get it cut the way Karen had. The style looked good on her and would be far easier for me at work. We did look alike ... I blinked and stared at my reflection. What was wrong with me? Why on earth would I want to look more like Karen than I did?

Huffing out a breath, I went into the closet, selected black slacks and a gray and black blouson top, and slipped my feet into my wedged walking shoes. It was nine-forty. I hurried downstairs hoping I had enough time for a cup of coffee. I couldn't face the day without one.

CHAPTER TEN

I took the elevator down to the main floor and made my way to the Breakfast Room. Mom, Marley, and the Duchess sat around the table finishing breakfast and discussing the previous night's outing. Great. If I could, I would bury that memory along with all the others I refused to recall.

"There you are, Marissa," Mom said as I entered the room. "You missed the others. They've gone off to do men things as your father put it. There's coffee in the urn."

She knew me well. I helped myself to a bowl of fresh fruit, topped with yogurt, and coffee.

"Did you enjoy yourself last night?" the Duchess, looking fresh as a daisy as if getting only six hours of sleep was normal for her, sipped her tea. "Both of your young men seemed quite taken with you. I recall the days when I had multiple beaus seeking my attention. You'll know which one is the one for you soon enough."

"It must've been the new look." I parried, not willing to dwell on the matter. My life would be fine without having to make that choice ... not that there was one to make. "I enjoyed the opera and the supper was delicious, although taking down my hair and washing off the makeup was a daunting task. There must be a hundred hairpins on the dresser in my room."

Marley laughed. "Knowing Remi, he probably plans to use just as many today."

Mom frowned. "I didn't realize you were returning to the spa." She raised her coffee mug to her mouth and sipped. "With all the other things you two have to do today, won't that create a time problem? Elise, didn't you say we needed to be downstairs before eight to welcome the guests?"

"Yes. I've arranged tea for four since supper won't be until ten. The men will get a bite at the club before returning to the house." She chuckled. "These formal events are so much easier for them."

I glanced from the Duchess to Mom and back again. What other things? I knew about the dress fittings, but I'd hoped to be able to sleep a couple of hours this afternoon if only to eliminate the bags under my eyes and fortify myself before seeing Ken and Karen again. At least Zak wouldn't be here—or would he? He wouldn't have traveled back to Knightsbridge last night. Refusing to dwell on that idea, I focused on my sister's answer.

Marley shook her head. "No. Since Louisa will be assisting Elise and Katie will be helping you, I've arranged for the team from *Shangri-La* to be here at five to help Rissa and me with our nails, hair, and makeup." She turned to me. "As a rule, I do my own toilette for day-to-day activities or Katie helps with my hair, but like last night, today and the main wedding festivities are too important not to look your best. Remi's very good at his job. He'll probably use those hairpins again. As he puts it, the style must stay for the duration."

I could get a ponytail to stay in place for hours, too, and without all the pins.

I shrugged. "Remi said that, did he? Amazing. All he did was tell me to be quiet."

She shrugged and nodded. "He's a bit of a perfectionist and really focuses on his work."

Could I talk him into something simpler tonight? Maybe a chignon or something I could manage on my own? Something with a lower metal content? I could ask, but my chances of success were limited.

As soon as I finished eating, Mom, Marley, Elise, and I headed out to the car where Austin waited.

The drive to the dressmaker's studio took no more than twenty minutes. He stopped the vehicle in front of a stone house with floor-to-ceiling display windows, showcasing extravagant and no doubt sinfully expensive ball gowns. Back home, women wore those types of dresses only for high school proms and weddings. Here, at least among the rich and titled, getting all gussied up seemed to be the order of the day. I vaguely recalled a time when people used to get dressed up for the theater or New Year's Eve, but like so many things that had changed over the years, the dress code was one of them. These days, people put comfort first, which was exactly the way I liked it. Give me a good pair of jeans, a comfortable pair of boots, and a nice top, and I was good to go.

"But you can do better than that, and you know it," my conscience prodded. I refused to listen.

I got out of the car and followed the others into the salon. I should've realized the process called the "final fitting" was going to take a while when Marley opened the door into what looked more like someone's living room than a store. A couple of sofas and stuffed chairs were situated next to tables across from a mirrored wall. There was no counter, no cash register, and no sales staff.

The wall opened, and a petite woman with glasses perched on the end of her nose entered the room. Behind her, in some strange procession, marched two men, carrying heavy trays, one with tea and coffee and an assortment of petits-fours, the other with champagne, orange juice, and flutes. I knew which drink I wanted. Alcohol might make the entire process more bearable.

Madame Denise, the Duchess's dressmaker, had created new gowns for her as well as those for the bride, the mother of the bride, myself, the other eleven bridesmaids, and the two flower girls, Emily and Imogene, who arrived shortly after us with their nanny. And Marley had called this a small wedding?

The two girls were the first to be fitted in floor-length, long-sleeved, white lace gowns trimmed at the waist, cuffs, and hem with sapphire blue ribbons. Since they stood still to be nipped, tucked, and pinned, it was obvious that they'd been through all this before.

Back in their matching outfits, the girls kissed their grandmother goodbye and left with their caregiver. I wished I could go with them. I would rather be anywhere but here. I finished my mimosa. The man by the tray offered me another. Knowing the day was going to be a long one, I opted for coffee instead.

It didn't take me long to realize that this wasn't the first fitting for Mom, the Duchess, or Marley. Elise went next, the assumption being that my fittings would take the longest. Great! I hated standing still at the best of times ... and having someone fussing around me would be sheer hell. The list of things I had to endure for my sister's happiness was growing by the second.

Elise followed Denise through the door in the mirrored wall. Mom and Marley settled on the couch once more, while I stood and paced.

"Marissa, for heaven's sake, sit down. How you can have so much energy after last night is beyond me." Mom sipped her mimosa. "You have a long day and evening ahead of you."

As if I didn't know that?

"Relax. You're supposed to be enjoying yourself. Have a macaron. They're delicious." Marley reached for a tiny chocolate goodie and popped it into her mouth.

I glared at the tray. Since the fruit hadn't completely dulled my appetite, I extended my hand toward a tiny pink cookie that reminded me of last night's cocktails. It melted in my mouth. I reached for another one. These things were like potato chips—you couldn't eat just one. I popped another into my mouth and moved away from the tray.

Was this how Madame Denise stayed in business? Did she ply her clients with fattening cookies and treats so that they would have to keep coming back to have their clothing adjusted? Not a bad business model. Knowing that I could easily consume every one of the luscious pink treats, I sat on a chair as far away from the tray as I could get.

While we waited for the Duchess to be fitted, a number of models came through the mirrored opening into the salon. The process reminded me once more of *Pretty Woman* and the scene where Edward had taken Vivian shopping.

"Who are they?" I pointed to the two women entering the salon once more.

Marley smiled. "Madame Denise's models. These are some of her new fall designs. When you do a lot of work with the public, appearances are important. Since I'll be taking on a more active role after Christmas, I'm going to need to update my wardrobe. These are some of the styles she thinks I might like."

The models came out two at a time. Sometimes, they wore day dresses, at others business suits, or casual wear. Mom took a shine to a chocolate brown suit with a box jacket while I rather liked the russet slacks with a tangerine top, but I'd never owned or even worn anything orange. The last time I'd seen anyone in and out of clothes that often, not to mention that quickly, had been when I was eight, playing with Barbie dolls, a phase that had lasted only as long as it took the family dog to chew the head off the doll.

When the Duchess joined us again, Mom went in for her fittings. The models continued to show off a variety of garments, and as much as dressing up wasn't my thing, it didn't take me long to appreciate Madame Denise's talent. Marley selected half a dozen outfits and the Duchess chose two.

I was on my second mimosa since the coffee had done nothing to settle my nerves when Mom came into the room, not dressed as she had been but wearing a gold and red sparkling sheath in an Oriental style that reminded me of Kate Capshaw's dress in the opening scene of *Indiana Jones and the Temple of Doom*. The fabric shimmered as if it were alive.

"It's perfect, Moira." The Duchess smiled. "You look wonderful."

"That dress is gorgeous, Mom. I've never seen anything like it."

She grinned. "Do you really think so? Madame gave me a couple of choices, but this one seemed so exotic. It's for tonight ... you don't think it's too much for a woman my age?"

My head snapped back, my jaw dropped, and I blinked. "You're only sixty. The dress is fantastic." Wow! People took their costumes seriously here. I looked at Marley. "Is yours that ... fancy?" It was the only word that came to mind. Last night's cocktail dress was the swankiest thing I'd ever worn. I couldn't imagine trying to pull off something even more extravagant.

Marley smiled and nodded. "Ours were delivered yesterday. Like you, Mom wasn't here for her final fitting last week. Don't worry. I picked yours out, and you'll love it. It'll be delivered this afternoon. Madame Denise only has to make the final adjustments to it. I can't wait to see you in it. I've got the perfect earrings to lend you to go with it. You're going to love it."

I nodded, not in the least reassured. "I'm sure I will," I lied. "Rachel was careful to get all of the measurements Madame wanted, so hopefully there won't be much to do. Besides, costumes don't really have to fit perfectly." I looked longingly at the macarons. Could I squeeze in another cookie?

Marley shook her head. "You're confusing a masquerade ball with a costume party. As a rule, there aren't any costumes per se, although some people might come dressed to match, in similar colors. A masquerade is the most formal type of ball you'll ever attend. The men will wear tuxedoes, usually tails, and the women will be trying to surpass one another with the most unique and lavish gowns money can buy. I have no doubt that Madame Denise's gowns will outshine them all."

I frowned. "Then why are they called masquerades?"

"Because you do wear a half-mask, the kind that covers the eyes and nose," Madame Denise added, handing Mom a feathered mask on a stick which my mother held up to her face. The colors on the mask matched the dress perfectly.

"They're like the ones you see in New Orleans at Mardi Gras. I opted for one I could take on and off at will, but I believe yours will be fitted to your face."

I had visions of a white plastic mask like the ones worn by the cast in the production of *Phantom of the Opera* that I'd seen a few years ago.

"Denise has created unique masks for each gown. Like your mother's, mine is on a stick, but Marley's is more of a headdress. I'd planned to host this event last spring." Elise reached for her tea. "But then we caught COVID, and the event was canceled at the last minute. I was quite excited when Aaron and Marley asked me to hold one to kick off their weeklong wedding celebration." The Duchess patted my hand. "You'll have a wonderful time, my dear."

Marley smiled. "You will."

"*Mademoiselle* Marley." Madame Denise helped Mom down from the box on which she'd stood to have the hem checked. "If you'll follow me..."

My mother turned away from us and headed toward the mirrored wall. Marley set her glass on the tray and followed.

"Wait!" I frowned. "Don't *we* get to see *the* dress?"

Wasn't oohing and aahing over the dress part of the pre-wedding ritual?

Marley grinned. "Of course. The Duchess, Solange, and the other bridesmaids have seen it, but you and Mom haven't."

Marley followed the dressmaker out of the room, and knowing I probably shouldn't, I grabbed another macaron and a third mimosa. Seriously. The glasses were small. How much alcohol could they possibly hold?

When my sister returned, I dropped into the chair, gobsmacked as a Brit might say. I had no words to describe how amazing she looked in the dress. Madame Denise described the gown as Marley slowly rotated in front of us. The bodice of the fitted white underdress was covered by a layer of spiderweb tulle with rose-embroidered accents on the shoulders and sleeves. The skirt consisted of three layers of crinoline covered by another three layers of chiffon. It brushed the floor in the front and had a flowing royal train behind.

"Her veil will be attached to the Habersham tiara, worn by all Habersham brides for centuries," the Duchess whispered.

"The single-layer veil, long enough to cover the dress's train is embroidered with the same rose pattern as the accents on the dress itself," Madame Denise finished.

Every bride was beautiful in her wedding dress, but my sister was stunning.

"Wow, Marley. Just wow. You look absolutely radiant."

Mom stood and held her arms out. "Darling you're the most beautiful bride ever. I can't wait to see the look on Aaron's face when you walk down the aisle on your father's arm." She brushed at a tear. "I've dreamed of this day ever since you were born. All parents do. They want to see their children happy and in love. All I need now are grandchildren." She turned to me. "Your time will come, Marissa. I feel it here." She held her fist to her heart.

I thought of the strapless, ivory, peau de soie wedding gown I'd purchased at a second-hand store five years ago, the one hanging in a garment bag in the closet back home. I'd fallen in love with its simplicity. All it did now was serve as a bitter reminder of my lost dreams. Perhaps it was time for me to sell it and forget that foolish nonsense. Not everyone got a happily-ever-after. I shrugged. This wasn't the time and place to face that truth.

Madame Denise addressed the Duchess. "Your Grace, the gowns belonging to the family and the rest of the wedding party will be delivered to Knightsbridge Thursday. I'll arrive Friday afternoon with a couple of my girls to help everyone dress and deal with last-minute glitches. Now, *Mademoiselle*, shall we remove your dress and move on to your sister? We have a lot to do in a short period of time."

I glanced at my watch. It was almost noon. How much longer could this take?

Mom and the Duchess rose. "We'll leave you to it. Austin will drive us back to the house since there are things I want to supervise personally for tonight, and Moira has agreed to help. Marley dear, don't forget. Tea will be at four. Do try to make it back in time since I would like your opinion on a few things."

My eyes felt large enough to pop out of their sockets. They expected me to be here for the next four hours? Impossible.

"I'm sure we'll be back in plenty of time," Marley answered before following the dressmaker out of the room once more.

Anxious but not wanting to appear so in front of the men who hadn't left our side since they'd come into the room, I sipped my mimosa, praying for the fortitude I would need to survive this. Would I be able to go through all this fuss on a regular basis? Not in a million years.

"Mademoiselle Kimble," Madame Denise came back into the room. "If you'll follow me, we'll get started."

With all the enthusiasm of a convicted man walking to the gallows, I followed her into the next room. Marley, now dressed in the camel slacks and chocolate shirt she'd worn earlier, sat in a chair.

"I can't wait to see the gowns on you."

She sipped from a champagne glass. Where had it come from? Thing One and Thing Two were still in the other room ... weren't they?

Shrugging, I walked over to the dressing screen where Madame and another woman waited. Until now, all I'd seen of the gowns I was to wear were sketches and fabric swatches.

I stepped around the screen, surprised by how much space there was back there. My jaw dropped when I saw the four dressmaker's dummies, one of them covered in a white cloth.

Those were my gowns? They were like something out of a fairy tale. I would look like a princess in them. Could I do them justice?

The first one was the demure, sapphire blue, chiffon sheath with elbow-length sleeves, and a square bodice embossed with seed pearls and crystals. That was the dress I would wear for the wedding. The blue matched the ribbons on the flower girls' dresses. Madame had me out of my clothes and into the dress in a matter of minutes. I slipped my feet into the matching shoes and walked out from behind the screen, stepping onto a small stage to have the hem checked.

Marley grinned. "What do you think?"

"It's gorgeous. Even though you sent me the sketch, I wasn't sure what it would be like. I love it."

With only a few nips and tucks, she pronounced herself satisfied.

Once again, I moved behind the screen. The woman helped me out of the gown I wore as well as my bra while Madame held the next gown for me to step into. This second dress, the one designated for the pre-wedding dinner, was a strapless olive silk with a built-in bra and a high waist pulled to one side under a bust and held in place by string tassels. The bodice sparkled with olive-colored sequins.

I stepped out to let Marley see me and allow Madame to nip, tuck, and pin to her heart's content. The drape on all of the dresses enhanced my figure. Neither of these gowns were the typical bridesmaid dresses no one would dare wear again, the kind that had been showcased in the movie *26 Dresses*. I'd been a bridesmaid once before and had resembled a lemon cupcake. Not this time.

The third gown, the one I was to wear for the wedding supper, not to be confused with the luncheon that would be served after the actual wedding, was a V-necked, sleeveless, red peau de soie with a fitted waist and a full skirt embossed with white floral appliqués.

"The dress I'm wearing is identical, but the colors are reversed," Marley explained.

"Are the other bridesmaids going to match me?" Not that I needed to stand out or anything, but I was curious.

Marley shook her head. "No one is going to match you. You're one of a kind, Marissa."

I was sure she meant that as a compliment, and yet ... Madame nipped and tucked once more before leading me back behind the screen.

"Well done, *Mademoiselle*. Your sister did say you weren't used to such things." She turned to the woman who'd helped me in and out of the gowns. "Rita, if you please, the mask is on my work table." She stepped over to the last mannequin.

While I was glad the entire process was almost over, I was curious to know what was hiding under the cloth.

"Is that my dress for the masquerade?"

"It is." She pulled off the cloth. "What do you think? Do you like it?"

I gaped at what had to be the perfect dress. "What's not to like?"

The midnight blue satin had a ruched bodice and featured a double-strapped one-shoulder neckline. A pleated band defined the Empire waist above a sleek, floor-length skirt with a leg slit that went well above the knee. Simplicity and elegance.

Quiet, unassuming, and yet ... the beauty of the gown shone through.

"It's incredible."

With Madame's assistance, I removed the red gown and slipped on the blue-black dress. The gown fit me like a second skin, highlighting my curves. When I moved, the fabric shimmered, going from black to midnight blue. As I had with all the others, I went around the screen to show Marley.

"I love it," I gushed, before she could say a word. "It's absolutely perfect. They all are."

Marley smiled. "I'd hoped you'd feel that way."

Madame Denise busied herself at the hem. A door opened and the girl she'd sent for the mask entered and handed it to her. The modiste stepped in front of me.

"The headband will hold it in place. Your hairstylist has seen the design and will know how to style your hair accordingly."

The mask began just before the crown of my head, and covered my eyes and part of my cheeks but exposed my nose and mouth. The feathers were a mix of deep blue and black, sprinkled with crystals that shone like stars in the night sky. I stared at the exotic, mysterious creature in the mirror. In this, not even my own father would recognize me.

"The gown will be delivered by three. Now, Let's get you out of this and into your clothing," Madame ordered. "I have a lot of work to do."

As much as I loved the gowns, I was glad the fitting was over. Glancing at my watch, I saw that it was after one. Perhaps once we got back to the house, I could sneak away for a quick two-hour nap before tea. That had been more dressing and undressing than I'd done since a short stint in the drama club back in high school.

When I came out from behind the screen once more, Marley thanked the dressmaker and hurried me out of the salon and back into the car that had returned for us.

"Ambrose's Austin, please." She got into the back seat. "I've arranged a light lunch for us before we move on. I know how cranky you can get when you're hungry and Anton will be ready for us at two-fifteen."

"Who's Anton?" She was right about my need to eat.

"He's the store manager at Harrod's. I called ahead and told him what we needed to save time. He'll have items ready for you in the right size. We didn't have time for Madame Denise to custom design everything for you. You need a few dresses and hats, at least for the race, the polo match, and the garden party."

I shook my head. "Marley, don't you think you're going a little overboard? Couldn't I just borrow something from you? I do have clothes with me, all of it new," I argued, although the only hat I had with me was the cap I wore running.

"You can't wear my clothes, and you know it, Marissa. I'm three inches shorter than you are with a much smaller bust. I had a look at your closet and most of what you brought is fine, but things are different here. I want you to fit in..."

"That's fine," I crossed my arms defensively, "but what am I going to do with all that when I leave? That stuff has probably cost more than I've made in the last two years. My life is simple ... not like yours. Those beautiful gowns..."

"Can stay here for your next visit. Madame will redesign them for you or remake them for me. Please, Marissa." Her eyes were so like Dad's green ones that all I could see was him admonishing me to play nice. "Let me do this for you, for us. Nothing will be wasted, I promise. Can't you at least meet me halfway?"

Halfway? This was all the way and more.

By four o'clock, I was so tired of putting on and taking off clothes that I was ready to scream— dresses, hats, shoes, gloves—it was a never-ending stream of garments and accessories. The only thing stopping me was the sheer bliss in my sister's eyes. Here I was, the sister she'd always dreamed I could be, enjoying the beautiful things she loved, not the hardworking electrician who dressed like a man to fit into a man's world. By the time the car returned and we collected all of the bags and boxes, I felt as if I'd dressed and stripped more often than Gypsy Rose Lee had at the height of her career.

Back at the house, Marley and I headed into the conservatory for tea. I didn't have much of an appetite. In our absence, the house had been decorated for this evening's festivities and dozens of staff bustled around adding the last-minute touches. Enormous bouquets of tropical flowers decorated the halls, the large dining room, and the ballroom. Peeking inside that room, I realized that the drapes had covered sliding glass doors, now open into the tent that had been erected earlier, easily tripling the area available for the masquerade. The space resembled a rainforest with massive tropical plants. At the far end, a mural of mountains, or was it a volcano, water gushing from it like a waterfall, added to the paradise the decorators had created. Tall tables, the kind you stood beside rather than sat at were sprinkled throughout the area. Inside the ballroom itself, an orchestra had set up for the evening, and tables of four or six replaced the usual furniture and had been set up around the dance floor. I'd been in reception halls that hadn't provided this much space for entertainment.

"What do you think?" Marley asked, coming up behind me. "The theme is an evening in paradise. I know I told you there were no costumes as such, but the masks reflect the theme. You like to watch from the shadows, while I've always embraced the spotlight. Tonight, you may want to be a wallflower, but it won't happen. I've made sure of that."

"You didn't have to, but I do love that dress. I know I'm not usually one for this, but thank you. You're not the only one who'll remember this week for the rest of her life. I will, too." I hugged her. "Come on. I want some tea before we have to get ready. You know me, if I don't eat..."

"Your stomach grumbles like a freight train." She laughed. "Let's go."

She put her arm through mine, and we made our way down the hall, admiring the gorgeous flowers, as we went.

The decorators had been at work inside the conservatory as several small tables were scattered among the plants. This would provide a quiet escape from the festivities if anyone wanted one. Maybe I could find a corner in here where I could hide for a while, but then again, behind that mask, wouldn't I be hiding already?

"There you are," the Duchess said. "You're just in time. Did you have a productive afternoon?"

Marley launched into a description of the dresses, hats, and shoes she'd insisted I needed while I dropped into a chair, every part of me wishing I could crawl into bed for an hour. I was exhausted.

"It was the best sisters' day ever."

I smiled. One person's pleasure was another person's torture, but hey, it was for a good cause. Marley was happy, so was Mom, and today, that was all that really mattered.

CHAPTER ELEVEN

I finished the last of my cucumber sandwiches—I was actually beginning to like the simple, airy snacks—even if they wouldn't fill me up the way a good meatball sub would. Megan came into the conservatory.

"Excuse me, Your Grace." The staff always addressed the Duke or the Duchess first when they were present. "The people from the *Shangri-la* spa have arrived. Jeeves has taken them upstairs."

"Thank you, Megan," the Duchess replied.

Marley stood, setting down her now empty cup of Earl Grey tea. "Take your time and finish up, Marissa. Remi can do my hair first. Ming can do your nails while he does, and then Sally can do your makeup while she does my nails."

"My nails?" I looked down at my garnet fingernails. "They're fine." I held up my hands. "I haven't even chipped one. Why would she have to do them again?"

She shook her head and rolled her eyes. What social gaff had I unwittingly committed now?

"But the color needs to be changed. Your nails should either be neutral or match your gown."

Who'd come up with that silly rule? Being a lady was both expensive and tedious.

"Really? I kind of like this color." I held my hand out admiring it.

The Duchess smiled indulgently. "It's the price we pay to be fashionable. I'll go up, too." She stood. "We'll all meet down here at say 7:30 for a little family time before the guests arrive."

I nodded and so did Mom. I shook my head as the doors swung closed behind them.

"If I'd known I was going to have to go through all of this to be Marley's Maid of Honor, I would've said thanks, but no thanks," I grumbled before finishing the perfumy tea. I wasn't really a fan of Earl Grey's blend. "I realize I should be grateful for all the trouble and expense she's going through for me, but I'm sure she has friends who would be highly more qualified to be her Maid of Honor than me, women who would actually enjoy all of this primping nonsense." I rolled my eyes. "It seems like such a waste of time and money. Who looks at your toes anyway?" Other than a pervert with a foot fetish.

Mom smiled, but I could see the disappointment in her eyes. As usual, I was falling short of expectations.

"Oh, Marissa. I love you, darling, but at times ... Not one of her friends could take your place. None of them is her big sister, and despite the differences between you, she loves you and always has. You're behaving just like you did the day of your prom. All I wanted to do was pamper you, and you carried on as if we were trying to skin you alive. I'd hoped you'd matured since then. Was that really twelve years ago?"

"Fourteen, but who's counting?" I mumbled.

I remembered that day only too well, and Karen's biting comment at the nail salon, "*Look who decided to pretend to be a girl.*" I'd shrugged, but the comment had stung. I hadn't been pretending to be a girl. I was a girl. If I did any pretending it was trying to find and prove myself in a man's world. I huffed out a breath, ruffling my lips in the process. It sucked.

"Well, I still like it just the way it is."

"I'm sure you'll get to wear it again, darling," Mom said, trying to appease me. "It sounds as if the floral dress you bought for the garden party has the same color in it. Now, go and play nice. It's just for the week. This is an important time in your sister's life. Can I count on you to at least pretend you're having fun tonight?" She glanced at her watch. "Look at the time. I need to get ready and so do you."

Once more, feeling like a long-suffering saint, I did my best to put on a happy face. When I got to my room, Ming was waiting for me. I could hear Marley talking to a man down the hall. I couldn't make out what they were saying, but it had to be Remi. He spoke to her even if he didn't talk to me. There was no sign of Sally and her magic trunk.

I opened the door and stepped inside. Someone had brought in a vanity table and two chairs. My mask was on the desk, waiting to be needed. Sitting like that, it looked like a glorious blackbird, with its shiny feathers swaying in the light. The Beatles song, "Blackbird" danced through my head.

Glancing inside the closet, I saw that all my new clothes had been put away. The dresses hung from fancy padded hangers, the three hat boxes were arranged on the shelf, and the shoes had been placed in the rack. Tonight's gown was beside the garnet cocktail dress. I grabbed my robe, knowing I would have to remove my top before Remi did my hair.

"I'll just go in the bathroom and put this on." Despite having undressed in front of countless women today, I was still shy about it.

Ming nodded and set her case on the table.

I went into my bathroom, removed my clothes, and dropped them into the clothes hamper, knowing they would be clean and hanging in the closet come tomorrow. After donning my robe, I took one last look at the gorgeous polish and went back into the room where Ming waited.

She'd emptied her case, removing nail dryers, nail polish remover, and an assortment of other bottles including polish.

"Please sit. I'll do your feet first."

"It shouldn't be as bad this time," I offered in apology for the mess my feet had been. "Do you know where I can get a bottle of the garnet polish you used yesterday?"

"Yes. I have it in my kit. I can leave it with you."

"That would be great." I might not put it on my fingers at home, but I could do my feet. "I can pay you for it," I offered.

"That's not necessary. It's already been paid for. Normally, we just keep them for the client, but I understand you aren't remaining in London. You're free to take it with you."

The girl smiled and sat at my feet. "I'm not giving you a pedicure today; I'm just changing the color of your polish."

Within a matter of seconds, she had the old polish off and went to work, redoing my toenails in an iridescent deep blue polish that would match my gown and sandals. I wasn't sure I was ready to have that color on my hands. Once she removed the polish from my fingernails, she buffed them. She surprised me by redoing them, not in the dark blue, but in clear polish, and sprinkling each nail with a small amount of glitter.

I smiled at her. "Perfect."

As soon as Ming finished, she left and within minutes, Remi stepped into the room with a basket full of brushes, combs, and sprays.

He examined the mask on the desk, measured the part that would cover my hair, and nodded. "You'll probably want to remove this after an hour or two. These flocked masks can be quite warm. Sally will make sure your foundation doesn't rub off."

I hadn't thought of that.

"I'm going to do something special tonight. Every woman will be envious, and I'll have them queued up around the block next week."

So I was going to be a poster child for Shangri-La. Why not? His business depended on rich, beautiful women wanting to be even more so.

To be perfectly honest, I hated having my hair done. For some reason, my scalp was super sensitive and brushing was usually a source of pain. With Remi, I realized it was different. He brushed my hair back from my face, without me wincing even once, and placed a line of hairpins across the top of my head as if he were building a fence. Fascinated, I watched in the mirror as he divided my hair into sections and began braiding from the line he'd created with the pins. Everything in front of that line would be hidden by the mask. Once the braids were complete, he wove them together. When he finished, he raised the large hand mirror to show me the lattice of hair he'd created, the highlights he'd added yesterday adding to the beauty of the design.

"It's amazing," I admitted. "You're very talented."

He smiled. "I know. I'll see you next week." The man gathered his implements and left me sitting there, staring at myself in the mirror.

I twisted my neck this way and that, trying to get a better look at the fancy weaving on my head, wondering if there was any way I could ever replicate it. The door opened, and Sally came in.

"Good evening, Miss Kimble." She examined my hair. "I've never seen anything so intricate. Not everyone's hair is suitable for Remi's weaving.

He's very fussy about that style. Let me guess. You must have a cap mask."

"Yes. It's on the desk. He mentioned that you would make sure my foundation didn't rub off on it. As far as my hair goes, I suppose that's why he pulled it all straight back tonight, although I often wear it like this—not braided but straight back in a ponytail." For often I could substitute every damn day.

The woman smiled and went over to the mask, examining it much the way Remi had. "And it suits you. Not everyone who wears their hair back should. Tonight, we'll make the eyes a bit more dramatic, and then focus on the mouth. Tell me about last night. How did everyone react to your new look?"

I chuckled. "Most people were as surprised as I was. Some didn't recognize me right away. I don't have time to go at it whole hog every day, but once in a while it might be nice to fancy myself up. I wish there was time for you to teach me a few tricks."

Sally nodded. "It's not all that difficult. What seemed like a vast change to you really wasn't. Let me explain what I'm doing as I go, and you should be able to do something similar on your own. But you won't need to be as heavy-handed with the eye makeup as I'll be tonight."

"You're serious? You think I can manage to do ... this myself? All I've ever used is tinted moisturizer, mascara, and lip gloss."

"Can you color?"

"You mean with pencils or crayons?"

Sally nodded.

"Of course. I used to color all the time as a child."

"This is no different. Think of your face as an image in a color by number set. Each area gets its own shade. You start by filling in the background and then you add the tones and highlights."

As she worked, she showed me how the planes of my face were divided.

"I can leave some of the products I use with you. Wanting to enhance what God gave you isn't wrong or being vain. Everyone wants to look their best. That's all you're doing. Just putting your best foot forward as it were. The thing to remember, especially during the day, is less is more. The last thing you want is for your face to melt in the heat."

She'd turned me to face her while she worked on my eyes.

"There. Have a look." She swiveled the chair to face the mirror.

Tonight, she'd applied a deep gray eyeshadow on the lower lids with a pearly finish that shone. My deep blue eyes looked darker.

"Watch what happens to your eyes when you put on the mask."

She went over, picked it up and brought it to me, setting it in place. The blue of my eyes popped against the blackness of the mask, and the bright red lipstick made my lips look more plump and kissable.

"Absolutely stunning. Miss Marley won't be the only one turning heads tonight."

"If I do, it has little to do with me and all the time and effort everyone else has put into this."

Sally placed several cosmetics on the table beside me. "This is all you'll need for a neutral daytime look. I've given you three lip colors, one on a peach side, another, a pink, and finally a mauve. Choose the one you like best. It doesn't have to match your outfit. It just needs to say, 'here I am. Look at me.' And smile. Work the right facial muscles." She removed the mask and put it back onto the desk. "Have fun tonight. I'll see you on Friday." And with that, she went out of the room, leaving me once more staring at the exotic creature in the mirror.

I couldn't begin to say how long I stared into the deep blue eyes of my reflection, but I jumped when someone knocked on the door.

"Come in," I called, expecting either Marley or my mother, coming to hurry me along.

"Megan," I smiled at the girl. "What can I do for you? If you've come to tidy up, they did a pretty good job of it on their own."

She shook her head, but I didn't miss the admiration in her eyes.

"Miss Marley sent these for you to wear tonight. She thought you might need someone to help you with your gown."

I grinned. I hadn't needed help getting dressed since I'd been four, but I could certainly use some help now.

I reached for the small box and set it on the table.

"I'm sure I could. I can't pull it over my head, not without making a mess."

Twenty minutes later, Megan zipped up the back of the dress.

I'd choked on my own saliva when I opened the box and saw the earrings Marley had sent.

"You look smashing, Miss Kimble."

I wore glittery dark blue sandals that matched the dress, elbow-length black gloves, and the sapphire and diamond earrings Marley had lent me dangled from my ears. I'd never seen anything as beautiful in my life. We were about to put on my mask when the phone rang. It was seven-fifteen. I had plenty of time.

I reached for the handset, wondering who might want me.

"Hello?"

"Miss Kimble, it's Clara. The photographer is early. Could you come down to the conservatory as soon as you're ready?"

While I hadn't met Clara, I knew she was the Duchess's assistant, and a lot of the preparations for this as well as the wedding had probably fallen on her shoulders.

"I'm ready, Clara. I'll be right there." I ended the call.

Megan helped me with my mask. The velour-lined item was soft against my skin, but I worried about being too warm and having all of Sally's hard work on my face ruined. Satisfied that I could see and wouldn't break my neck, I opened the door into the hallway and gasped.

"Marley! Oh my God! You look amazing."

She stood there in a strapless, A-line, deeply low cut, sleeveless gown, shining and shimmering in the deep teal of a peacock, his tail up for all to admire, the gloves and headdress mask as well as whatever she'd put on her skin to make it glisten completing the look. Her lips were coral with a gold sheen to them.

"You look wonderful, Rissa, just like I knew you would. Let me see your hair."

I turned so that she could see the lattice of braids. Her own hair had been straightened and flowed down her bare back, the dress having none above the waist.

"I'm speechless. It's gorgeous, not that I can figure out how it's staying in place. Crazy Glue? No one will look at anyone else when you're in the room."

She laughed. "I wouldn't be too sure of that. You look pretty spectacular yourself. As for staying in place, not quite glue but there are tabs stuck to me as well as to the dress. Look carefully, there's spider web tulle dyed to match my skin all over my back. It just looks bare. The dress won't go anywhere, but I'm anxious to see Aaron's face. You're the first one to see it. I wanted it to be a surprise."

"Well, it's absolutely gorgeous. A peacock in paradise. What could be more perfect?"

I put my finger up to call the elevator, but she stopped me.

"You have to believe I didn't know about this earlier today. I found out after tea. Dad and Aaron decided that you shouldn't be unaccompanied tonight. Aaron has a few male relatives who are, well ... randy, for lack of a better word. They try to collect bedmates at these affairs and they don't all subscribe to the 'gentlemen don't tell' model. You are brilliant, but you can be quite naïve. You'd be a lamb going to slaughter with those wolves."

I wasn't quite the rube she made me out to be, but then the truth hit me. My heart plummeted into my stomach. There was only one reason why I might be upset.

"Let me guess. Zak was there. You did say he was Aaron's special guest. Did he offer or was he coerced into doing it? Never mind. It doesn't matter. Ken will be here. I will be allowed to leave my keeper's side, won't I?"

Either circumstance would hurt.

"Of course you will. It's not like that—"

Before she could continue, the elevator door slid open. Two masked men in tails stood there. I recognized Zak's build and his beard as well as the shape of the lips I'd once known so well. He stepped into the hall to let Aaron out.

The man's cleanly shaven jaw dropped. "Darling, you look ... stunning," Aaron said, his mouth gaping, as he examined the dress. He swallowed awkwardly. "Is that ... is that dress secure?" He stepped out of the elevator, and placing his arm across her shoulders, pulled her aside. Had Marley's surprise been too much for Lord Broadmere?

Zak stood closer to me.

"Once more, you leave me without words, Marissa." He glanced at Aaron and Marley. "It looks as if there might be trouble in paradise. Shall we go down? They may need a few minutes."

I glanced over at Marley who stomped her foot.

"Maybe." I chuckled, trying to sound blasé when the entire mess was tearing me apart. "Smoke and mirrors, a magician's trick to make you see what you want to see and not what's really there. He may think the dress is too risqué, but having met Madame Denise and knowing Marley wouldn't do anything scandalous in front of Mom and Dad, everything will work out. As for me, when you have this many people determined to make you into something you're not, eventually, you quit fighting and simply play along. Reality will set in soon enough, and I'll be back in my coveralls, wiring someone else's fancy house."

He pressed the button for the first floor. "This really isn't our world, is it?"

"No, and honestly, I wouldn't want to live like this. It's far too complicated. There are so many rules ... You do look rather dapper though."

He grinned. "I look like the plastic groom on someone's wedding cake. I've never had so much trouble getting dressed."

I laughed at the wedding cake ornament comment since oddly enough, it did fit. At least dressed in deep blue, almost black like this, no one would mistake me for the bride.

The elevator doors opened. He held out his arm to me as he'd done the previous night.

"They're waiting for us. Let's go and make the bride and groom's excuses." He turned to face me so that I could see his eyes and the earnest truth in them. "I promise to step aside when Ken arrives. I saw how you two were last night. I want you to be happy Marissa. It's all I ever wanted. Just think of me as more of that smoke and mirrors illusion you mentioned. And if he makes you happy ... Ken's a great guy. He's been through a lot."

But I was happy with you, until that night...

I'd forgotten to ask Mom about Ken's accident and this didn't seem to be the place to do so. Not knowing what else to do, I put my arm in the crook of his and let him lead me to the conservatory.

The second we walked into the sunroom, I was bombarded with the oohs and aahs of those already there. Solange was resplendent in a pale yellow chiffon Grecian gown with a matching mask. Mom wore the gorgeous red and gold gown she'd tried on this morning, while the duchess was in a chiffon trumpet dress with a high neck that started out deep pink and ended in the palest shade of the color at the floor. Her mask was covered in the same sequins as the bodice of the dress. Like Mom, she carried her mask. She also wore a bandeau tiara.

"Is that the tiara Marley will wear for the wedding?" I was impressed by the gorgeous piece of jewelry.

"No, this one belonged to my mother, the Duchess of Eastwick. I must say that gown suits you beautifully," she added. "Denise outdid herself." She looked around. "Where are Aaron and Marley?"

"Right here," Marley answered. "I had to prove to Aaron that the dress wasn't going to slip off at the wrong time. In addition to the sticky tapes on the side, it does have a flesh-colored tulle along the back. My hair hides it."

"And I fell for the illusion," Aaron admitted. "Marley never ceases to amaze me. I look forward to many years of surprises from her. I still can't believe she agreed to be my wife."

I stood next to Zak, inhaling the scent of his cologne, or was it his pheromones, and wishing the last five years had never happened. To be in his arms again, to feel his lips on mine, his body hard against mine would be paradise.

"She takes it all in stride, doesn't she?" Zak nodded his chin toward Marley, pulling me out of my dream.

I nodded. "She always has. She was everything they wanted in a daughter, while I was ... different."

"You were unique, gifted, and a hell of a lot smarter than the Barbie wannabes. Never for a minute think that any one of them was better than you."

But you chose one of them over me.

"Your Grace," a dark-haired woman in an elegant white pantsuit entered the room with a couple of photographers. This had to be Clara. She carried a tablet and was scrolling through information on it. "Some of the guests have arrived early." She said it as if it were some kind of major social faux pas. "I've asked them to wait in the lounge. If we could get the society page photograph, we can move on to the receiving line."

"Of course, Clara. It's no problem. We're all here, now." She turned to the photographer. "How would you like us to stand?"

Marley and Aaron were in the center, with the Duke and Duchess next to Aaron and Jacob and Solange beside them. Mom and Dad stood beside Marley, with me and Zak next to them. It was the traditional wedding photo pose. He took several pictures with masks and a few without. Zak's hand burned against my waist, and his breath seared my neck, filling me with such longing that it was a chore not to lean into him. At the Duchess's urging, the photographer took pictures of each couple together. Finally, he was finished, and we were free to leave the conservatory, but I and my shadow weren't going very far.

With my arm in his, we moved to the ballroom and stood at the entrance. The Duke and Duchess first, then Marley and Aaron beside Solange and Jacob. Next were Mom and Dad and finally Zak and me at the end of the line. I watched Marley like a hawk, nodding politely when I was introduced to someone, holding out my hand when it seemed appropriate, and repeating each name as Jeeves announced it. Not one name would stick I was certain of it, and I would be saying 'my lord and my lady' to people all evening.

It didn't take long for me to appreciate that Dad and Aaron had been right when it came to some of Aaron's friends and cousins, several of whom would be in the wedding party. The leers on the face of some of the viscounts, earls, dukes, and barons made me grateful Zak was there.

"Count Louis de la Forêt," the butler announced, "the Countess Marie-Louise de la Forêt, and their son Paul-Emile."

Solange stepped forward and embraced her father and mother, speaking to them rapidly in French. My French was good, but not that good. Her brother said something, and Solange removed her mask and glared at him. He shrugged.

"Papa, Maman, these are Mitchell and Moira Kimble, Marley's parents, and this is Marissa her sister, and Dr. Zakary Mitchum, her escort."

"Ah, yes, the Canadian veterinarian who looks after Aaron's horses," the Count said, shaking Zak's hand. "I should have you come to the château while you're in Europe and check out my bloodlines. We'll talk later. It's a short flight and I can send my plane for you."

I bowed to the countess. "Madame la Comtesse, *c'est un plaisir de faire votre connaissance.*"

The woman smiled. "*Le plaisir est le mien.*"

The Count reached for my hand and raised it to his lips, kissing my glove.

"I see that beauty runs in your family, Mademoiselle Kimble."

I nodded my head. "*Merci, Monsieur le Comte.*"

He smiled. "I hope you'll keep a dance for me this evening."

"But of course."

Surely the Count wasn't one of the people I was to avoid?

"And you can keep a few for me, *ma petite.* After all, once the wedding takes place, we'll be almost family." Paul-Emile reached for my hand.

The man wore a crimson mask that matched the waistcoat of his tuxedo and the sash across his chest.

I felt Zak stiffen by my side.

"We black sheep of the family have to stick together. Solange was telling us about your little job. It must be nice to get away from the mundane and frolic with the *beau monde*."

He released my hand, and I rubbed it on my skirt before the next person came down the line. I would do my best to avoid being alone with the man. He might be Solange's brother, but he was trouble with a capital T.

Leaning back into Zak, I whispered. "I guess that smarmy guy is why you're here. Thank you. I'll do my best to stay away from him, family or no family."

"I'm always here for you, Rissa."

I turned back to the line, praying it would end soon. My feet were killing, me and I needed to use the loo.

"Whoever made your gown and Marley's is an absolute genius," Karen said. She wore a navy gown with a wide boat neck that showed off the ample cleavage she'd purchased at school although I thought the few pounds she'd gained might have enhanced it. She carried a navy feather and sequin mask on a stick. The crystal pendant and earrings completed her look. She frowned. "Zak? My goodness, it is you. When I heard your name, I was certain it had to be a mistake, but I would recognize those gray eyes anywhere. So have you two kissed and made up? That's wonderful, although Ken will be so disappointed."

Zak smiled. "Ken has nothing to worry about. I'll step aside when the time comes. Where is he?"

Karen looked behind her. "He was here a minute ago." She turned to the man beside her. "Let me introduce my escort, Dr. Matt Tanner."

"Pleased to meet you, Miss Kimble, Dr. Mitchum. I've heard a lot about you. I look forward to seeing you without your beautiful mask. Karen tells me you two used to be mistaken for one another. I find it hard to believe another woman could be as beautiful as her."

Gag me with a spoon.

Karen reddened. "Matt and I talked a lot about the past. Ken should be along soon. Don't forget, we need to talk before you go back to Canada."

She and her date moved on and I turned back to the seemingly endless line of English nobility. How much longer would this go on?

CHAPTER TWELVE

Twenty minutes later, when Clara arrived to announce the end of the formal receiving line, I could have kissed her, or at the very least fallen to my knees and worshipped her. My feet were killing me, and my face itched. It wasn't actually warm in the ballroom, but thanks to my nerves and Zak's proximity, I was sweating like a pig, praying my deodorant wasn't going to let me down.

Zak followed the men to the bar, and I made a beeline to the water closet off the kitchen, the one I knew the guests wouldn't be using tonight. Mrs. Brown and her staff were too busy preparing the smorgasbord for later in the evening to see me slip into the room. The minute I locked the door, I removed my gloves and mask and inhaled deeply, pleased to see that my face looked exactly the way it had appeared earlier. Whatever Sally had sprayed onto it to keep everything in place certainly worked. Once I attended to business, instead of replacing the mask and gloves and going into the ballroom to join the others, I slipped out the kitchen door I'd used before and went out into the backyard.

Night had fallen and the air was fresher than it had been. I inhaled deeply and slowly exhaled letting go of all the tension from the day and the last hour. The garden was awash in fairy lights and the glow from the tent. Here and there, muted conversation proved I wasn't the only one who'd sought to escape. I walked along the stone path, the gravel crunching under my feet, hoping no one had found the secret bower I considered my refuge. I hadn't seen Ken arrive, although Karen had said he was here somewhere. If he was, he couldn't be too anxious to find me. Maybe that was a good thing. My emotions were screwed up, and I didn't know how I felt about anything, least of all the two men recently reintroduced into my life.

With Marley socializing and my mother's curiosity about everything and everyone, I figured I had half an hour before anyone would get worried about me. Zak might wonder where I'd gone, but I assumed the Count had him cornered somewhere discussing horses and bloodlines. I brushed at the seat to make sure it was dust-free, placed my mask and gloves beside me, and sat down.

Hidden by a stand of bamboo, my hidey-hole was no more than three feet from the back of the tent. I could hear the muffled sound of the music from the ballroom and the muted crash of water tumbling from the fake waterfall a few feet away from where I sat. The lack of sleep last night, the day's running around, and the stress of the last hour got to me. I closed my eyes. Years ago, I used to sit outside on a clear night, stare up at the stars, and let Mother Nature soothe me.

I opened my eyes and looked up. Whatever stars one might see in London were few and faint.

Closing my eyes once more, I leaned back and focused on the sounds of nature. There they were. Crickets chirping, talking to each other. Were they talking about the day's activities, what they had planned for the future, short as it might be for them? I imagined a whole conversation...

"Have you seen him yet?"

A man's voice coming from inside the tent startled me out of my semiconscious state. I didn't recognize the British voice, but it was vaguely familiar as if I'd heard it recently.

"He was quite angry with you. You didn't exactly pick the best time to tell him all that."

I sat up. How long had I been hiding here? I hadn't worn my watch. The last thing I wanted to do was eavesdrop on a private conversation, and it sounded as if I'd inadvertently stumbled onto one that could prove embarrassing for someone. I stood and reached for my mask, but one of the gloves fell onto the ground. I stooped to retrieve it, grateful for the slit in the skirt that made it possible.

"No, and that worries me. I didn't expect him to react the way he did. I knew he might be annoyed, even upset ... My timing wasn't the best, but I don't want to see him hurt again. He's suffered enough."

I stood, glove forgotten. I knew that voice all too well. Karen. Who was *he*?

"I should've kept my mouth shut and let the chips fall where they may, but I've been carrying this guilt around for five long, miserable years. I came to England to escape it, but you can't escape your past. It follows you everywhere. They say confession is good for the soul. That may be, but while I might feel better, I didn't expect Ken to be so angry. I thought he would understand why I didn't say anything sooner. What he said ... Damn it! He lost his leg because of me and my damn smart-alecky mouth." Her voice choked on the last words.

Ken had lost a leg? My God! Why hadn't he mentioned that? I dropped onto the bench once more. Tears brimmed my eyes, and I fought to keep them back. I'd been hurt and angry that night five years ago—I still was—but I'd never wanted anyone to die.

"Sweetheart, we've all done things we aren't proud of." In my mind's eye, I saw him pull her into his arms. "We've talked about this. You have to let it go. Admitting what you did or didn't do is one way, but forgiving yourself is another. That night, you were angry and frustrated. Regardless of how a relationship ends, both parties feel the pain of loss. I might not have been there that night, but from what you've said, I can imagine two blokes as drunk as they were and a house that reeked of vomit and stale beer wouldn't have helped the situation. When people are miserable, they don't see straight. They want others to be just as unhappy as they are. They don't think things through. Unfortunately, it's simply a law of physics. For each action, there's an equal and opposite reaction. He pushed your buttons, as it were, and you pushed back. You can't put yourself inside someone else's head and guess how they'll react. If she'd really loved the man, don't you think she would've given him the benefit of the doubt?"

"Do you think I haven't asked myself that question a million times since that night? I should've known she would flip. She wouldn't recognize sarcasm if it bit her on the ass. For her, everything was black and white, positive and negative. There was no gray, no grounding wire as she might say. She saw something, she interpreted it, and I let her believe what she wanted to. Any other woman would've jumped into the water and scratched my eyes out, but not the Ice Queen. She walked away."

I gasped and covered my mouth, afraid they might hear me. What did they say about eavesdroppers not hearing any good things about themselves? I should leave and go back into the house, but how could I? I was stuck here as surely as any rat in any trap.

The man chuckled. "I realize that I don't know her, and no doctor should offer a diagnosis without examining the patient for himself, but to have risen in her field as she has, she has to be strong-willed, determined, and level-headed, willing to make sacrifices, all with the end game in mind. A woman can't succeed in a man's world without drive and ambition. If she was ready to believe the worst, then maybe she didn't love the guy as much as she thought she did. Maybe what you did was give her the excuse she'd been waiting for to get away, not just from you, but from everything, and to strike out on her own without anyone or anything holding her back. I gather from what Ken said that she's done quite well for herself."

Tears slid down my cheek. Were they ruining my makeup? I didn't give a damn. Yes, I'd done well, but at what cost?

"Since coming to the UK, you've done everything you can to be a better person than you were, and I love you for it," he continued. "Give Ken some space. In time, he'll realize that it was all an unhappy happenstance. He wasn't responsible for her flight, and neither were you. People have to face the consequences of their actions. Drinking and driving that night was his choice, a costly one that could've been far worse. He learned from it and turned his life around. Marissa made her choice the night she left Cedar Lake. Was it the right one? That's up to her to decide. As far as Zak is concerned, it seems to me that if he'd really wanted to find her, he could have. Licensed professionals have to be registered somewhere. Even if she went to work in a different province, that information had to be available. Something held him back, too."

I should go inside and confront them, demand that she explain herself, and tell Matt that he was wrong. I'd loved Zak with every fiber of my being. I hadn't been looking for an excuse to leave everyone and everything I loved—I'd been forced to do so. Zak was the one who hadn't felt the same way, the one who'd turned to my competition, just as I'd feared he would.

My breath caught. Could Matt be right? What did they say about being so convinced that something bad would happen that it did? I was so sure that Karen would find a way to take him away from me, just as she had every other thing I'd coveted over the years. Could I have misinterpreted what I'd seen that night? It had seemed so obvious, but what if what I thought I'd seen had simply been the product of a self-fulfilling prophecy? I'd been tired. Zak and Ken had been drunk...

No! I wouldn't jump to conclusions again, because if I did, it would mean accepting responsibility for destroying our relationship. I needed time to think, time to examine this new theory, time to talk privately with Karen and learn the truth, as painful as that might be.

I stood, ready to escape into the water closet to check that my tears hadn't destroyed my makeup when I heard Ken's voice.

"Karen, have you seen Marissa? Everyone is looking for her. She's been missing almost an hour."

Damn! I'd been gone too long.

"No. The last time we saw her was in the receiving line," Karen answered, in control of herself once more given Matt's interpretation of that night, one I'd never even considered. "Maybe she's gone off somewhere with Zak, and they've made their peace."

I hadn't asked what kind of doctor he was, but I would bet on psychology or psychiatry. He seemed to understand people's behavior from the inside out, even better than they might understand themselves.

"I doubt that. He's talking to the Frenchman, Jacob's father-in-law," Ken answered. "He provided the wine and champagne for this little shindig. Marley said she headed toward the kitchen when the receiving line ended, but none of the kitchen staff recall seeing her. Aunt Moira went up and checked her room, but she isn't there either, and neither is her dress and mask, so we know she hasn't run away again. By the way, I didn't make it to the receiving line in time since I was stewing in my own pudding as it were. What was she wearing?"

"A gorgeous, midnight-blue sheathe and a black and blue feathered cap with a mask attached. Her hair is up in an intricately woven braid design.

Believe me, she looks fantastic. It really made me regret cutting my hair short, but at the time I thought it would help." She sighed. "Knowing Marissa, she has a bolt hold here somewhere. A hiding place where she can disappear for a few minutes to recharge. She's always hated this kind of thing, and we both know it," Karen stated. "Remember the prom? She disappeared for a good hour. Where did we find her? Inside the school library, reading a damn book about circuits. God. Why was I always so mean to her? Seeing all the heartbreak when people lost siblings to the virus, I realized that she was the closest thing I had to a sister. Sadly, in my envy and jealousy, I pissed it all away."

Karen had been envious and jealous of me. I found that hard to believe. She'd been the popular one with all the friends while I'd been the oddball.

"This place has to have a library," Matt said. "Let's start looking for it. If she's not there, then we can try the conservatory."

"Good idea," Karen agreed. "I'm sure one of the staff can point us in the right direction."

"Of course," Ken added. "In fact, one of them might know if there's another spot she could've found."

"Are we friends again or do you still hate me?" The concern in Karen's voice was real.

Ken chuckled. "You're my twin sister. I could never hate you, no matter what a bitch you can be. None of us is perfect. We were drunken jerks that night and nobody poured that booze down our throats. When you were explaining everything earlier, I was as mad at myself as I was at you. I'd like to say everything that happened afterwards was your fault, but that would be lying to you and to myself. I'd really liked Marissa, and well ... Some of the night came back to me. I may even have recalled some of it when I saw her in Brockton, and she mentioned that horrible Ice Queen nickname I gave her."

"Ice Queen? Interesting name, but from what little I saw of her, I don't see it," Matt said. "I see a beautiful woman who's shy, doesn't like being the center of attention, and yet endures what she must for the sake of others. I have no doubt that standing there in that line tonight was difficult and painful for her. It would've been quite interesting to see her face behind that mask. It should come as no surprise that she's escaped for a bit. Back then, she would've been conflicted since wanting to succeed in a man's world would've been difficult. It still is. Society has come a long way, but there are still those with definite ideas about gender roles."

"Yeah." Karen's voice was husky. "When we were younger, we did everything together, not always by choice, mind you ... There were times when our mothers even dressed us the same. We might've teased and squabbled a bit, but we were always the Three Musketeers as Dad called us."

Ken chuckled. "Those were the good old days. But, once we hit high school, she changed. After you got the head cheerleading position instead of her, she started distancing herself from us. I don't think I realized that until tonight. She fought tooth and nail to be her own person and worked her ass off, getting top grades, basically avoiding or ignoring the things you did, Karen. When Zak moved to Cedar Lake, Marissa blossomed. He might've been my friend, but I hated the way she looked at him and how happy they were. When he proposed, and she accepted ... Maybe I was a little in love with her and never realized it. That might even be why I was harder on her, teasing her more because I wanted her to look at me the way she looked at him. In my drunken state, I might even have imagined she would turn to me for comfort. I may even have made an offer ... I never expected her to leave. As much as I care for her now, she needs to know the truth about that night as does Zak. Once everyone knows what really happened, for better or worse, we can move on. Right now, she and I are friends. Can it be more? I don't know, but until everything is out in the open, I don't want her to learn about my leg. The last thing I need or want is her pity or to be her second choice. Once she knows what really happened, she and Zak can decide where to go from there. Until then, I'm going to sit on the sidelines and wait to see how the game unfolds. If she turns to me ... well, I won't say no. Now, let's go and find her before Aunt Moira has a coronary."

I stood there transfixed as reality set in. Guilt filled me. I should rush out there and apologize to them for my shameless eavesdropping. Whatever had happened five years ago had been my fault, not theirs. I'd reacted emotionally, not waiting to hear the truth. My phone had blown up with calls, but I'd destroyed the SIM card instead of checking them. As much as I might want to run away again just as I had that night, lick my wounds, and try to figure out what had happened, I couldn't. I had to shove this pain down as deep as it would go, put on a happy face, and get back inside with a plausible excuse for Mom and Marley before I ruined the night for them.

Karen wanted to talk to me. I had to be willing to listen to her and give her the opportunity to explain. Something bad had happened to her that night, too. Until I got to the bottom of things, I had to carry on as if nothing had changed. Could I do it? I was a lousy actress at the best of times. It wasn't a matter of could. It was a matter of must. I swiped at my face, pleased when nothing seemed to come off it onto my hands. I put on my mask and my gloves and retraced my steps to the kitchen door, hoping the water closet would be empty.

"Miss Kimble, there you are," Clara said, her voice filled with censure as she waited to see who else would come through the door. Did she think I'd snuck outside with one of the randy aristocrats? "Everyone is looking for you. Miss Marley wants to introduce the wedding party."

"I'm sorry. I was in the tent and then decided I needed a breath of air. I'll go in right now." I stopped. "I assume they're in the ballroom?"

The woman seemed surprised by my answer.

"They are."

"Thanks." I reached for a glass of champagne off a waiter's tray. "I'm on my way."

As soon as I was in the hall, I downed the glassful of bubbly and placed the empty glass on a tray headed into the kitchen, before reaching for another full one.

All black or white, positive or negative? Not anymore. I was moving into the gray area and staying there—even if I needed to be a little tipsy to do so.

I'd just stepped into the ballroom when the Duchess saw me. She put down her mask.

"There you are, dear. Marley has everyone searching for you. Where have you been?"

I couldn't lie to the Duchess. There had to be a law or at least a rule against it, but I didn't have to tell her the whole truth.

"Outside in the garden. It's no secret that this isn't my usual kind of affair. I was feeling overwhelmed and needed a break. I didn't realize ... I fell asleep." I shrugged.

She smiled. "Let me guess. You found my bench behind the bamboo. It's my favorite spot in the entire yard. I shall miss it dearly when we move to Knightsbridge. I'll have to have Evans find a way to create my green bower there. I know there's a great deal going on in your life right now, and some of it seems overwhelming, and I can understand your need to take a breath, but we'd best get in there before my future daughter-in-law decides to send for Scotland Yard."

I chuckled. "She does get a little overly dramatic at times." And I didn't? No. I just threw the baby out with the bathwater and ran away. "After you, Your Grace."

I followed the Duchess deeper into the room until we were standing behind my parents and Marley. The Duchess winked and walked away. I finished the second glass of champagne.

"Clara said you were looking for me."

Marley and Mom jumped up as one.

"We were so worried, darling. Are you okay?"

"I'm fine, Mom. I just needed some "me" time."

"Marissa, where have you been?" Marley hissed. "I was afraid you'd run off again."

The best defense was a strong offense. "Why on earth would you think that? I wasn't aware that I had to check with you before I left the room."

"That's not what I meant. It's just you vanished—"

I shook my head. I didn't want to lie, but right now, the truth wouldn't serve me well whereas...

"I did not vanish. I needed to go, you know, and I didn't want to do that in the water closets the guests were using, so I went up to my room for "me" time. That took a while. I've been a little irregular since I arrived."

"For God's sake, no one wants to hear about your potty habits," Marley snarled, looking around to see who else might've been listening.

I didn't care who was. All I wanted to do was get her mind off my disappearance. Topics like that always made Marley uncomfortable. I recalled all too vividly how upset she'd been when Mom had brought home three Robert Munsch books. *Smelly Socks*, *I Have to Go*, and *Good Families Don't*. She loved the stories, but I couldn't read them to her if anyone else was around.

I reached for a glass of champagne from a passing server's tray. Three glasses in quick succession would certainly loosen me up. After this one, I should take a break and find some water.

"Did you need me for anything in particular or are you simply monitoring my location?"

I was laying it on thick, but I had a lot to process, and since I couldn't do it, the last thing I wanted to do was answer questions about it.

"I want to introduce the wedding party to the people present. Most of them will be at the wedding, but there are a few who can't make it. How easy is it for you to remove your mask?"

I thought of the tears I'd shed in the garden. I'd meant to check my face in the water closet before Clara had waylaid me.

"Well, it's quite hot under here, so the makeup may have melted or something." I took it off once more, praying my face wasn't a disaster. "What do you think?"

"It'll do. Come on." She stopped. "Where's Zak?"

"The last I heard, he was talking to Solange's father." That was the truth. "Why do you want Zak? You told me he wasn't in the wedding party."

Marley shook her head ruffling the feathers of her headdress.

"He isn't, but he's your dance partner. I suppose in a pinch we could ask Paul-Emile, but ... The groomsmen and my bridesmaids aren't couples. They each have a partner here. My other attendants are women I work with at the embassy, and Louisa Bolt, the ambassador's wife. The exception is Lady Celia. She's Aaron's cousin. I sent him to find her since I've never seen her. She's a professor of something or other and lives near the Scottish border. He likes her, but I think the rest of the family find her odd. He asked me to include her if I could, so I did. I would do anything for him. I haven't even met her yet, but like you, she sent Madame Denise her measurements. I'm trying not to panic. At any rate, I want everyone to be dancing and then, I'll have them stop the music, call up each of my bridesmaids, and introduce her." She stopped speaking and her mouth split into a grin. "Here comes Ken. I'm sure he'll be willing to help out. Stay here while I gather the others." She hurried away.

I smiled as he walked over to me. He'd removed his mask and carried it in his hand. Unlike most of the men in tails, he wore a regular tuxedo, but he looked every bit as handsome as the other men in the room. His limp was more pronounced tonight and guilt ate at me. Not only had he danced a lot last night, but he had also walked back to his hotel. He might not want me to know about his missing leg and prosthesis because he didn't want my pity, but was it pity to simply care about a friend?

"No mask?" I smiled.

"The damn thing doesn't fit right. It must've been made for someone with a larger nose. Marissa, you look incredible. I'm sorry I missed the receiving line earlier, but I was ... occupied with something else. It's all been taken care of now."

He hugged me quickly before releasing me and stepping away, his actions a far cry from the way he'd held me yesterday. Was he really pulling the plug on a romantic relationship with me?

"You look very nice yourself." If he wanted to just be friends, that was fine. There had been no sparks last night when he'd kissed me, but I wasn't going to lie to him or anyone else if I could help it. "I heard about your leg. That must've been one hell of an accident."

"Never drive drunk. It was a tough lesson but even harder on the elk I hit. I'm fully recovered and as functional as I'll ever be, but a whole lot smarter." He shrugged. "I'd hoped you wouldn't find out so soon."

"Why not?" I challenged. "We're friends, aren't we? Aren't friends supposed to care about friends? Is it bothering you tonight? I'd hoped to add you to my dance card."

"Nothing would stop me from dancing with you." He grinned. "Certainly not an artificial leg. I'm damn near bionic. I come with interchangeable parts. I have one for swimming and another for jogging. I even have a special one with boots for skiing. I would beat you down the hill this time."

I laughed, glad to see the return of the camaraderie we'd established in Brockton.

"Maybe. I'm in pretty good shape. I'd give you a run for your money, but I haven't skied in five years."

"I did notice your shape. I'm gimpy, not blind." He winked.

I smirked. Some things never changed. "Since Zak isn't here, maybe you could be my partner. Marley wants to introduce the bridal party by plucking us out of the crowd as it were and calling us up onto the stage. You know my sister. Everything had to be a grand production. Like this masquerade ball. Back home, we'd just have a barn dance with everyone in comfortable, casual clothes."

"But then I would miss wearing this penguin suit and seeing you in that exquisite dress. I forgot how long your legs were, although I do remember getting a good look at them the last time I saw you. No wonder you were a track star."

I rolled my eyes. "Track star? I tripped over the last hurdle and lost the race."

"Maybe, but you looked great at practice." He wiggled his eyebrows.

"There you are, Rissa," Zak said, appearing by my side. "I looked for you after the receiving line, but before I could find you, the Count cornered me to talk about his mares. If Marley hadn't rescued me, I'd be there still. She said something about a special dance?" He turned to Ken, smiled, and extended his hand. "Hi, Ken. I saw Karen and her doctor friend in the receiving line. Glad you made it."

Ken reached for the hand. "So am I. I wouldn't miss this for the world. It's not every day that I get to hang out with the rich and famous." He smiled at me. "Now that Zak's here, I'll claim a dance later."

Marley returned. "Okay. Now, everyone knows to get up to dance when Aaron and I do. He should be here any second. He just went to get ... there he is."

"Professor Sykes? Celia?"

Ken's shocked voice startled me. The awe on his face had me turning around to see who had captured his attention. Whoever it was meant something to him, something important.

CHAPTER THIRTEEN

The petite brunette by Aaron's side looked up and smiled. Her deep brown eyes behind large wire-framed glasses opened wide before narrowing in discomfort. Like Mom, her mask was a hand-held one that hung against the skirt of her lavender Empire-style gown. She wore less makeup than most of the women here, and while her fingers were neatly polished, her nails were short like mine had been before Ming had changed them, and painted mauve to match the gown. Her hair was pulled to one side in a cascade of curls held in place by a silver and amethyst comb that matched her earrings, necklace, and the ring on the third finger of her right hand. Was it an engagement ring? Somehow I didn't think so. Hadn't I planned to wear my old one as a means of scaring away the Lotharios? Kindred spirits often recognized each other in the strangest ways.

"Ken." She licked her mauve-painted lips. "This ... this is a surprise—a pleasant one, of course. What ...what are you doing here?"

"You ... look amazing." He stared at her as if a miracle had unfolded before his eyes. "Marley and her sister Marissa here," he moved closer to me and put his arm around my shoulder as if I were his old army buddy, "grew up in Cedar Lake together. She's the electrician I mentioned last week when we were discussing those resistors. Marley invited my sister Karen and me to tonight's masquerade. I didn't expect to see anyone else here that I knew." He smiled broadly. "It's great to see you."

The woman's gaze took in how he held me, and her eyes clouded slightly. "I see. I didn't realize you had friends and family in England. I'm sure my mother must've mentioned that Marley was from Alberta. It slipped my mind."

"And I didn't realize you knew Aaron." He frowned. "Small world."

I moved out of Ken's grasp and stood closer to Zak before holding my hand out to the woman.

"Lady Celia," I said, deciding that I might have the opportunity to play Cupid here. If something positive could come of this night, I would be a fool not to grasp it. "I'm Marissa Kimble, Marley's sister." I pointed to Marley who stood there transfixed at the turn of events. "It's nice to meet another working woman. What Ken failed to mention is that he, his sister, and I were all born on the same day and are more like family than friends—you know, brothers and sisters and all the rivalry that goes with it. But how do you two know each other?"

Ken's gaze was still on the brunette, his brow wrinkled. "Lady Celia—I didn't know she was a peer—and I work on the same green energy project in Newcastle. Does everyone know about your title other than me?" There was a touch of hurt in his question.

She shook her head. "No one knows except you. It's not a secret or anything. I just don't use it in my professional life." She shrugged, her cheeks reddening. "It's a pleasure to meet you, Marissa." She shook my hand firmly before turning to Ken once more. "Maybe we could keep it between us? People look at me differently when they realize who I am. I hope that won't happen between us. I enjoyed sharing the occasional lunch with you and discussing the project. At any rate, Aaron and I are first cousins," she explained, "and since I'm the family spinster, the one they've been trying to marry off for years despite my proclivities toward earning my own living, your friend Marley was forced to put me in her wedding party. That's why I'm here ... to be paraded before the Ton once more in the hopes that some titled scallywag who wasted his fortune will be desperate enough to consider marrying me so that I'll produce the required grandchild and return to my rightful place as Lady Celia and forget the rest."

Aaron coughed and smothered a laugh. "Celia has quite the sense of humor although I doubt my aunt appreciates it."

I burst out laughing. I liked this woman and a blind person could see that Ken did as well. Judging by Lady Celia's reaction, she wasn't immune to him either.

"We working women should get together and chat about the pitfalls of that kind of life," I stated. "I'm not royalty, but not everyone, including my mother, appreciates the lifestyle choices I've made."

"I'd like that," she smiled. "I was exaggerating—just a little. Perhaps we'll have time to chat at Knightsbridge. I'll be arriving on Thursday. I can't get away any sooner." She looked at Ken. "We have the presentation on Wednesday."

Marley interrupted. "The orchestra's ready. Celia, where's your partner? I want everyone up dancing."

"I'm sorry, Marley," she answered not looking in the least bit sorry, and maybe a bit defensive.

I didn't blame her. She didn't really want to be a part of this. If I didn't have to be, I wouldn't either. I couldn't imagine being dragged around to affairs like this in the hopes that some loser earl, baron, or some other title would need money badly enough to marry for it and not love which didn't seem to be part of the equation. What was wrong with her parents? If she was a professor working on this project, she had to be brilliant.

"I ... I don't have a ... partner. I came because my parents insisted on it. I'm not planning to stay long. After the introduction, I'll leave. Perhaps my uncle or your father would dance with me if I must be dancing."

"Please stay, Celia, or should I say, Lady Celia," Ken spoke up before anyone else could. "If you'll let me, I'd be honored to be your partner. Besides, you haven't met Karen. I know I've spoken of her often enough to bore you to tears."

She smiled, her eyes shining brighter than they had.

"Celia is fine, Ken. I appreciate the offer. I rarely have a white knight riding to my rescue, but don't you have a companion?"

He grinned. "Nope. I came stag, too. I was hoping to meet someone special tonight. It seems I have. Don't worry about the leg. With the adjustments you made, it's working better than ever. Shall we dance?"

"I'd like that."

Marley grinned. "Excellent, but not quite yet. When you come on stage, make sure to have your mask on, and then you'll remove them after the entire bridal party has been introduced. That'll be the signal for everyone's masks to come off. It'll be time for supper." She exhaled heavily, joy oozing from her pores. "Won't it be fun?"

Lady Celia looked at Ken and smiled. "Oh, yes. This will be great fun."

Ken nodded. "Definitely."

I should probably be upset that he'd essentially dumped me for another pretty face, but in this case, I was happy and relieved. Based on his comment, Celia not only knew about his prosthesis, she'd worked on it. Fate might just have done me a favor. The music started and Zak reached for my hand. "Shall we?"

I nodded. This was going to be fun? I wasn't quite as sure of that as the others were.

* * *

By midnight, I was as keyed up and stressed as I'd been earlier in the evening after I'd overheard Karen, Ken, and Matt. In the back of my mind, looming over me, like one of the anvils that always landed on the coyote in the cartoons, was the information she'd revealed. Each time I danced with Ken, listening to him praise Lady Celia and her accomplishments, I was pleased for him but felt a sense of dread eat at me, slowly eroding the false front I wore. If what had happened that night hadn't been what I thought it was and my actions had somehow contributed to Ken's accident, then wasn't I responsible? If that was the case, then the entire calamity that had befallen me was my fault. It seemed as if the choice I'd made that night might not have been the smart one I'd considered it to be even though I'd gone on to greater things. I owned my own business, was financially secure—and as lonely as I could possibly be.

I ached in Zak's arms, and yet, each time he asked me to dance, I accepted. I'd never considered myself to be masochistic, but how could I deny that now? We couldn't talk about that night since Karen hadn't shared the truth with him, and I only knew the tidbits I'd overheard. I tried to relax, smile, and enjoy the wonder of being with him once more, but I couldn't, remaining stiff in his arms, lest I give in to temptation and melt into him. Could I forgive him? The better question might be, could he forgive me? Could I forgive myself?

The smorgasbord Mrs. Brown and her staff had provided earlier had been excellent, but I'd only picked at my food, something both Zak and my mother had noticed. I'd fended off their curiosity by shrugging.

"I pigged out on the cucumber sandwiches at tea. Besides, my system isn't conditioned to eating this late."

As Zak and I moved around the less-than-crowded dance floor, many of the older guests had left, I noticed Ken and Celia moving together over on my right. They were talking, laughing, and obviously happy in each other's company. Given the opportunity, those two might grow to be more than work colleagues. I hoped so. I wanted things to go well for Ken. He deserved to be loved and so did Celia. We all did. No one should have to settle for second best.

"Are you upset about that?" Zak indicated the couple with his chin.

"Ken and Celia? Good grief, no. I think it's wonderful. Ken and I had a great time when he visited me in Brockton, but we're more like family than anything else—that's probably why the three of us fought so much as kids. Sibling rivalry. I resented them for everything from hijacking my birthday to preventing me from doing what I wanted to do or thought I did. I'll bet they felt the same way. What our parents considered cute and expedient was really frustrating for us. Things just got worse as we got older." I shrugged, realizing that it was the truth. We'd wasted so many years fighting and trying to one-up each other. "You're an only child. Things were different for you. After Marley was born, I was envious of her, too. I didn't even try to be the kind of big sister she wanted, brushing her off as the pest she sometimes was. I'm hoping that all this will somehow make it up to her. Time is an incredible teacher; unfortunately, it takes a lifetime to learn its lessons."

"You're being too hard on yourself."

"Am I?" I was about to apologize for leaving the way I had five years ago when the music ended.

"Sorry for intruding, Marissa," Karen said as we stepped off the dance floor. "I really need to talk to you and Zak. It's important. I didn't realize you were leaving London in the morning and flying home the day after the wedding. I thought we'd have more time."

Certain that I knew what she wanted to discuss, I nodded.

"Is there somewhere private we can talk, someplace where we won't be interrupted?"

"We can talk in my room," I offered, knowing I could count on no one disturbing us there.

"Okay. That works. Matt is in the conservatory, talking to Aaron and Uncle Mitchell about ranching in Canada, so I doubt he'll miss me for a few minutes. Ken is seeing Celia off. I like her. She'll be good for him—not that you wouldn't be." She looked away. "Here he comes now."

She hurried over to her brother and spoke to him.

He frowned but nodded and followed her over to us.

"Lead on. I suppose this is as good a time as any to clear the air. It'll make everything easier in the long run."

For him maybe, but I had my doubts.

Zak furrowed his brow. "Clear the air about what?"

"About what happened five years ago," Karen said.

I nodded. "We all have unanswered questions about that night. This way."

I picked up my mask from the table and walked out of the ballroom, Zak, Ken, and Karen following me. The hallway was deserted. I called the elevator and the four of us entered, no one daring to speak, the weight of what was to come of this all but crushing us in our own way. I pressed the button for the third floor.

When the doors swished open, I crossed the hall and opened the door to my room. Megan had cleaned up the remnants of the earlier activities.

"Sit wherever you like." I swept the room with my hand.

Ken dropped into the wingback chair. His leg had to be bothering him. I sat on the side of the bed. Karen took the chair in front of the vanity.

"I'll stand," Zak said, leaning against the door. "Karen, what's the point of all this? Why rehash that night now? Better to just forget it ever happened and move on."

"Because we can't move on without the truth. Look at us. We're together and yet there are impenetrable walls between us, walls that should never have been there in the first place because I lied to you all about what happened that night."

Zak straightened. "What do you mean you lied? Lied about what? I screwed up somehow, argued with Marissa, and she broke off our engagement. What more is there to say?"

Karen heaved a sigh. "Well, for one thing, you and Marissa didn't argue. In fact, I doubt you said ten words to her. Matt has asked me to marry him, and I don't want this on my conscience any longer. Let me start at the beginning. I was in a miserable mood that night. I'd been dating Dr. Kellerman at the hospital and had caught him in the supply closet with another one of the nurses. Somehow, I managed to get through my shift, but when I got home, I was at the end of my rope. The house was a pigsty and you two were drunker than skunks. I made myself a rye and coke and because you asked for one, I made you each one which was essentially just cola. I left you two on the couch watching a ballgame and went to my room."

"Sorry about the breakup and the mess we made, but while my memory of that night is fuzzy, I do recall having too much to drink. I don't see what that has to do with Marissa and me." Zak's voice betrayed his frustration.

Karen huffed out a breath. "Way more than you realize. I'd just undressed and had opened the bedroom window to let the night air in when I heard a splash. I looked out and saw someone's bare ass floating in the water in the hot tub. As drunk as you guys were, I was afraid whoever had fallen in might drown."

I gasped. Zak had been the one in the hot tub.

"I rushed out of my room, not bothering to get dressed," Karen continued. "Ken was out cold on the couch, Zak's puke-covered clothes were beside the recliner where he'd been sitting, which meant he was the one in the hot tub."

"I don't recall going outside, but I did wake up naked," Zak admitted.

Karen nodded and continued. "I rushed out. You were still in the hot tub, but you'd managed to flip over so that your head was above the water. You tried to get out, but drunk and off balance, you couldn't. I was afraid you might go under again, so I jumped into the water and helped you up onto the side, getting dunked a few times in the process. Trying to get you out was like trying to wrestle an alligator. I'd just gotten you seated on the side of the hot tub, your back leaning against the fence, and I was resting my head against the side, trying to catch my breath before getting out myself when you mumbled, *I love you, Marissa.* I recall saying something like *sure you do, asshole, but I'm the one who just saved your sorry ass, not Marissa* when she screamed your name. My head snapped around and there she was, outraged, the perfect ending to my absolutely rotten day. I couldn't help it ... call it exhaustion, relief, stupidity, it doesn't matter, but I burst into a fit of giggles."

Suddenly, I was no longer in my bedroom but in the yard that night.

Over the sounds of Blue Rodeo, I could hear the bubbling of the hot tub. The yard was littered with red and blue Solo cups and beer cans, proof that there had been one hell of a party here. I turned the corner and stopped cold. The pool deck and patio were deserted, but not so the spa area.

A woman, naked at least from the waist up, her long, wet hair streaming down her back was kneeling in front of a naked man sitting on the edge of the tub, his back against the wall, his head thrown back, his eyes closed, his ... I started to back away until the bells and whistles exploded inside my addled mind, and I recognized the mole on the man's shoulder.

"Zak!" The word exploded from me.

He opened his gray eyes, blinked, and smiled. The woman stopped what she was doing and turned to look at me. Karen.

"What the hell do you think you're doing?" I screamed.

She giggled. "I would think that was obvious."

Zak's eyes opened wider and his forehead creased. "Rissa? What are you doing over there?"

The door into the house slid open. "What's all the yelling about?" Ken took in the scene. "Oh shit! Karen, for God's sake, put something on."

Standing tall, hurt beyond words, but refusing to give in to the pain, I stood my ground.

"It's okay. I'm just leaving. It seems Zak isn't quite ready to go."

"Lighten up, Rissa, for God's sake," Ken said, slurring his words, proof that he too was drunk. "It's only a blow job. You two aren't married yet, and despite his desire to shackle himself to the Ice Queen, he does have some heat running through his veins and other places. Maybe he wanted a warm woman for a change instead of one determined to wear the pants in the relationship. I, on the other hand, am open to experimenting."

"Not with me. Allow me to make it easier on him and your sister." I pulled off my engagement ring and threw it at the couple in the tub, the platinum and diamond ring scarcely making a sound as it plopped into the bubbling water. *"If she wants him, she can have him. This Ice Queen is out of here. All of you can enjoy what's left of the party."*

"So that's it. I was angry, frustrated, and upset. I'd just saved his damn life and instead of thanking me, you assumed I'd been giving him a blow job and threw your engagement ring at us. I might've been a lot of things back then, but the fact that you thought I could stoop that low really hurt.

"I ... I don't know what to say." Tears rolled down my cheeks.

"Why didn't you tell her the truth?" Zak asked, his face pale. "Why did you lie the next day and tell me we'd had a fight? We looked all over for that ring. You knew it had gone into the tub ... you let me think I'd said something ... Why, Karen, why?"

"Because I was hurt and angry. By the time I got you back into the house, she was gone. I called her cell phone and left messages explaining the whole damn thing, but she refused to return my calls. So, yeah, I was pissed and lied to you. If that was the way she wanted to be, fine. It wasn't until Aunt Moira told me they couldn't reach her either that I considered the fact that she might've destroyed her phone. Like her mother, I expected she would just be gone for a few days, but then the days turned into weeks and months, the phone number was no longer in service and her Facebook profile was gone. Then Ken had his accident and I blamed myself. After that night he was drinking more heavily, you'd stopped being friends, and for the first time, I understood why Marissa had run away." She looked at me. "I asked your mother for your new number, but she said she couldn't give it to me, not unless she wanted to lose you forever. Once Ken was out of the hospital, I couldn't stay in Cedar Lake. I blamed myself for all of it and I was too ashamed to tell the truth. I joined Billie and

April and came here to London. I met Matt at the hospital when I was taking care of his mother. One thing led to another, and we're here, but along the way, I spoke a lot about home. When he asked me why I'd left, it all came tumbling out. I'm not proud of what I did. I regret it—well, not saving your life Zak, but everything that happened after. I wouldn't have said anything if we hadn't all ended up here together. Then, listening to Ken talk about clearing the air with Marissa and realizing the two of you had never patched things up ... Matt's a brilliant psychologist. He said you needed to know the truth and now you do. I'm not asking for forgiveness, just understanding. Had you come back to Cedar Lake, all this would've come out sooner. I'm not blaming you for running, Marissa. I did the same thing when I came here."

Ken spoke for the first time. "I learned all this earlier tonight and I was mad as hell when I did, but I can't let Karen take all the blame. I was drunk, but I said those hurtful words and for what it's worth, I jumped to the same conclusion you did, Marissa. I'm sorry."

Zak leaned forward. "I suppose I should thank you for saving my life, Karen, but I can't quite forgive you for the rest of it. And the same goes for you, Ken. That you could jump to that conclusion shows how little you knew me, but Marissa, the fact that you thought I could betray you like that. Obviously, what I imagined we had wasn't real. Love without trust isn't love at all. If you'll excuse me, I'm done for the night."

"Zak, I ... I'm sorry. It wasn't..." I didn't know what to say. There was no undoing the damage I'd done that night.

He looked at me, hurt and sorrow branded on his face, and without another word, opened the door, and left. I stared at the door, tears coursing down my cheeks.

Ken came over to me and touched my shoulder. "We'd better get going, too. I don't know if Karen's confession has made things better or worse. Maybe when he thinks it through..."

Karen stood. "Marissa, I do have one question. Why did you never respond to any of my messages or Zak's?"

"Because I never got them. I saw the missed calls when I got home, but I was so hurt I didn't want to hear any excuses. I turned the phone off and destroyed the SIM card," I admitted, tears continuing to fall. "While neither you nor Ken were blameless, you weren't the one who ruined everything. I did that all by myself. Zak's right. He was the only innocent party, and I didn't trust him, but more importantly, I didn't trust that what we had was real. I ran away because I couldn't bear the pain of failure. I had no phone and no Internet service for more than a month. I created a new Facebook for myself under the name of Shocking Experience, primarily for the business." I stood. "Thank you for saving his life and for telling me what really happened. If I hadn't been so quick to jump to conclusions ... I do forgive you. I might even understand why you did it. It grated on my nerves when someone called me by your name ... I certainly understand what a broken heart feels like. I hope you and Matt will be happy together. Will I see you at the wedding?"

"I'll be there," Ken said, "as Celia's date." He smiled. "That woman impressed the socks off me, but I thought she had a fiancé. She wears that ring ... I'm glad we're friends, Marissa, but I don't think we were meant to be anything more than that. I believe you know it, too." He came over to the bed and hugged me. "Once Zak thinks things through, he'll see that everything happens for a reason. He still loves you, and I know you still care for him. Just give it time. You're going to be together all next week."

"Unfortunately, I won't be there," Karen said. "Matt's proposal means he and I are flying to Switzerland to break the news of our engagement to his parents and get the ball rolling for our own wedding. I hope you and Zak can find a way to work things out. Like Ken said, I can see the feelings you had for each other are still there. It may not happen overnight, but if it's meant to be, it will be. I learned a valuable lesson that night and try to think before I speak. And once again, I'm sorry that my foolish pride caused so much trouble. Now, I'd better get downstairs before my fiancé comes looking for me."

I nodded. What more was there to say?

They left the room. Robot-like, not thinking about anything I was doing, I removed my gown and hung it in the closet, used the cleanser I found in the bathroom to remove my makeup, and with my hair still in its intricate braid weave, crawled into bed. Zak was right, without trust, there couldn't be love. Rolling over, I cried myself to sleep, weeping for the lost dreams of the past as well as those of the future.

* * *

It was almost eleven when I went downstairs the following morning, dressed in the outfit Marley had chosen for this afternoon's trip to the races. I needed coffee in the worst way although the analgesics and the shower—I hadn't washed my hair and it was still in braids—had helped me feel a bit better. The tears I'd shed had left me empty but determined to put on a happy face for Marley. I'd even made an effort to slap on some makeup and didn't look as bad as I felt.

When the elevator doors opened, I noted that several bags and suitcases stood by the door. I'd left one of the countless servants whose names I couldn't remember packing up my stuff for the trip to Knightsbridge via the race track. I wore a mauve and white flowered dress, and carried a white purse to match my shoes as well as a silly little feather thing for my head that was highly unlikely to prevent sunstroke.

"There you are Marissa," Marley said. She wore a coral dress with a matching jacket. A fascinator made of starched, coral ribbon and tiny, white flowers sat on the table beside her purse. "You look great and your hair will be perfect for your hat. Sometimes, Remi's styles can last a couple of days. Did you enjoy yourself last night?

The evening was a huge success, and the Duke and Duchess are thrilled about Celia and Ken. Are you ready to admit that dressing up can be fun?"

I smiled, keeping my feelings buried deep inside. Fun was the last word I would use to describe the evening.

"It was eye-opening to say the least, and the dresses ... it's a night I'll never forget. Ken and Celia look happy together. He doesn't have a title, but if he makes her happy, does it really matter?" I looked around the room. "Where is everyone?"

"Mom and Elise are checking their rooms to make sure they have everything, Aaron's out in the garage—we're driving down in his car to give you more space in the Bentley. Several of the servants who are accompanying us to Knightsbridge have already left, but if you want breakfast other than fruit, yogurt, and coffee, someone can make it. The Duke is in his study—he had a call to make before we leave. And, you'll probably be pleased to know that Zak left for the airport early this morning.

Apparently, there was an emergency on one of the farms back home."

I gaped. This wasn't what I wanted. I needed him here where I could talk to him, explain why I'd been so ready to believe the worst. He had to know that I'd loved him then, that I loved him now. The question was, did he love me?

CHAPTER FOURTEEN

Determined not to ruin the week for Marley, I shoved my emotions deep inside me. In the Bentley, Mom and the Duchess gushed about how wonderful the evening had been. I gave them the answers they wanted, but I was sure the Duchess could see through my fake smiles.

The races were interesting, and I did my best to pretend to have fun. I flirted with a few of the single peers I'd met the previous evening, making sure not to encourage them in a pursuit doomed to failure. With the help of one of the barons, a consummate gambler, I made small bets on who would win the race, who would place, and even came out on top, the man claiming I had an excellent eye for horseflesh.

Whatever I'd learned had been at Zak's side all those years ago.

I was grateful to Marley for insisting I dress up as I had. In my flowers and feathers, I was able to blend into the crowd, chat now and then, and yet stay on the outside, allowing Marley all the glory and attention.

When the races ended, we continued on our way to Knightsbridge. The guest house where my family would be staying was almost as large as Renfield House had been. There were five servants on hand to see to our needs. After dropping off our luggage, we proceeded to the main house a few hundred feet away. I'd expected a grand house, but this was a castle with towers. The only things missing were a moat and a drawbridge. We entered through massive front doors and then indulged in a fancier tea than we'd had in the city. I didn't have much of an appetite, the whole day weighing heavy on me, so when I got the opportunity to escape, I took it and walked back to the guest house.

My bedroom was huge, with its own modern bathroom. From my window balcony, I could look over the fields and forests. A road snaked through the grasses and trees and called to me. I hadn't jogged since my arrival and now, despite the activities of the day, I needed to run.

Like it had at Renfield House, the phone on the desk in my room connected with the kitchen in the main house.

"Yes, Miss Kimble," a man said. "How may I be of service?"

"Hello." Would I ever get comfortable with this? "I was wondering how much time I had before supper."

"The Duchess has requested the meal be served at eight-thirty, but if you require something now, I'll be happy to get it for you."

"No, that won't be necessary. Thank you." I ended the call. That gave me three hours. My luggage had been unpacked, so I changed into my running gear, set the timer on my watch for forty minutes, and made my way downstairs, stopping long enough to tell one of the servants that I was going for a run. The last thing I wanted was Mom and Marley panicking because I wasn't in my room.

The country air was fresh and cooler than it had been in London. I didn't know the area, but as long as I stayed on the road and didn't turn off anywhere, I should be fine. After stretching, I set off at a low steady pace. At first, I cleared my mind and focused on the sounds of nature. I could hear birds singing, insects buzzing, and here and there something scurrying in the brush. When my timer went off, I was relaxed and in control of myself.

On the way back, I thought about everything that had happened five years ago and yesterday. There was nothing I could do about it now. My job this week was to be Marley's Maid of Honor, and I would do it to the best of my abilities. For once, I would put aside my own wants and needs and embrace the girliness she adored. I would be the sister she'd always wanted. Then, once the festivities were over, I would return home to Brockton, sit down, and take stock of my life.

By the time I got back to the guest house, my muscles were screaming, and I was covered in sweat. Up in my room, I took down the braids, chuckling at my wild look. I showered, washed my hair and conditioned it, and then rinsed off and dried myself. I opened the closet and selected the other dress I'd purchased from *The Oasis* back home, a sleeveless red A-line with a scoop neck. I pulled my hair back with combs and took time to put on foundation, eyeshadow, mascara, and the pink lipstick Sally had given me. Then, I added the pearl earrings that I'd inherited from my grandmother. The whole process really hadn't taken all that much time. I might not wear it for work, but maybe it wouldn't be such a bad thing for my downtime.

When Dad knocked on my door to tell me the car was here to drive us to the main house, I was ready.

The cook at Knightsbridge was every bit as knowledgeable as Mrs. Brown had been and for the first time in two days, I was starving. The multiple-course meal was delicious and consisted of cold cucumber soup, followed by Beef Wellington and roasted asparagus. The next course was a purple cabbage and blood orange salad, followed by a savory of deviled eggs, something that somehow felt odd and out of place considering the order in which we ate our food back home. Next came a selection of cheeses, and finally, the best carrot cake and cream cheese icing I'd ever tasted. Just when I thought I couldn't eat another bite, the servants brought out tea and coffee as well as a selection of fruit, truffles, and petits fours, including the macarons I'd adored at Madame Denise's salon. Each course had been served with its own wine, and by the time the meal ended, it was eleven o'clock, and I was drowsy.

Instead of walking back to the house as I'd done this afternoon, I got into the car with Marley and Mom and Dad.

"Breakfast will be served here in the morning, but we're expected to be ready to go to Baroness Kingsford's garden party at one," Marley said. "There will be all kinds of food there. I plan to skip breakfast and sleep in, but the rest of you do what you like. Dad, you might want to visit the stables. They're around back. You can't miss them. I understand you're going hunting in the afternoon. I think Aaron mentioned something about pheasant or grouse. Feel free *not* to kill anything. It's a barbaric activity at the best of times."

Dad chuckled. "Yes, dear."

"I think I'll sleep in, too." I laughed. "I've had enough to eat tonight to last me two days. I don't want my gowns to require a lot of adjustment. I'll see you in the morning."

After kissing Mom and Dad, I went up the stairs to my room. I undressed, hung my dress, and put on my short nightgown. The window in my room opened onto a small balcony. I stepped out into the cool night air and looked up at the sky awash with stars the way it had been in Cedar Lake, suddenly homesick for the mountains and trees of Alberta. Sighing, I went back inside, closed the door, and crawled into bed, praying for a dreamless sleep.

* * *

The ride to Baroness Kingsford's home took half an hour. Solange, Jacob, the girls, and their nanny had arrived earlier this morning while I'd still been sound asleep. They were staying in the castle itself. The two older girls were competing at the gymkhana on Wednesday, something I was actually interested in seeing. Aaron and Jacob were both on the same polo team and had a game tomorrow, something else we were all supposed to attend. To me, polo was more or less croquet on horseback. I understood the game, but really didn't see the point of it, but then again, I wasn't a fan of golf either. Give me softball, basketball, football, hockey, even curling—anything with a little physical exertion and action.

Over the next few days, the other members of the wedding party would arrive so that everyone would be here on Friday for the rehearsal and the dinner to follow. If the meal was anything like what we'd been given last night, I would have to watch myself or my blue dress wouldn't fit for the wedding.

As we drove through the English countryside, I admired the beauty of the land. We drove through a couple of quaint villages where life seemed to move in low gear. When we arrived at the Baroness's home, instead of the orderly polite reception I expected, the place was in chaos. The butler showed us into the salon where the Baroness sat on the sofa next to her daughter. The empty glass on the table told its own story.

"Mama, please, pull yourself together. The Duchess is here," the young girl dressed in pale blue sat next to the distraught woman who had to be the Baroness.

"Good grief, Natalie," the Duchess said. "What on earth has happened?"

"There's no power in the kitchen, Your Grace," the girl explained. "Montrose, our handyman, isn't here, and Wiggins doesn't know what's wrong or how to fix it."

"Without power, the kitchen can't prepare the tea and the food," the Baroness wailed. "The garden party will be ruined. I'll be the laughingstock of the Ton. I won't be able to show my face at any of the soirees and Melissa here was all set to have her coming-of-age party this year." The woman wept and then blew her nose loudly, all pretense at decorum gone.

I couldn't help chuckling although I did my best to muffle it behind my hand. This had all the makings of a farce.

"Natalie, pull yourself together," the Duchess ordered. She turned to me. "I know you probably have no experience with our electrical grid, but do you think you could have a look? Perhaps if we could figure out what the problem is, I could call Knightsbridge for assistance."

"Of course, Your Grace. I'd be happy to."

Baroness Kingsford's head snapped up. "What good would that do? I'm ruined, I tell you, simply ruined."

"Natalie, calm down. You're behaving like a spoiled child. We'll figure out a way to solve this problem. If we can't have tea, we'll have wine. Most of the ladies will be fine with that. You've obviously had a tipple or two already. Marissa is an electrician in Canada. Let her at least have a look."

The woman nodded, but her gaze remained skeptical.

"Where's your fuse box, my lady?" I removed my white gloves and the straw hat I'd worn and handed them and my purse to my mother who stood rooted to the floor, her eyes huge as she watched the drama unfold.

"Wiggins can show you," she answered, not because she had any faith in my abilities, but because she didn't want to refuse a higher-ranking peer.

"This way, miss." The man led me out of the salon and down the hall to the kitchen. The staff was bustling, some making sandwiches, others icing cakes. The items waiting to go in the oven sat on the counter. Unlike Renfield House, this grand home didn't appear to have been modernized. "If you prefer not to go down there, I can tell my lady that you did. I doubt there's anything you can do. Montrose warned her this might happen, but the Baroness never does anything preventative. This isn't the first crisis we've had with the electricity this year. There's no point in ruining your clothes."

Typical man. I hated the assumption that I couldn't do something because I was a girl. There was a good chance I could fix the problem or at least identify it so that with the right equipment someone from the castle could. It wouldn't be the first time I worked on an antiquated system, but the circumstances where I would find myself wouldn't be ideal.

"You're right about the clothes. Can you find me a pair of overalls and some boots, size seven or larger? I can get by with shoes that are too big, but not too small. And then, can you tell me where I might find Montrose's tools? Since there's a good chance I can fix this, don't you think I should try?"

I was sure that I saw a glint of admiration in the butler's eyes. Within ten minutes, I was out of my dress and wearing a pair of mechanic's coverall with oil and grease stains on them and a pair of heavy work boots only a size too big. I felt like my old self again. In Montrose's workroom, as neatly organized as mine back home, I found all the tools I used at home for a job of this sort. With a large LED flashlight in hand, I followed the butler down the stairs to a damp, smelly basement, fairly certain that I knew what had caused the problem.

"Are there mice or rats down here?" I looked around, dodging large spider webs as we walked along the stone hallway. I didn't like rodents, but I despised spiders.

"There are several different species in the region. Montrose does his best to trap them, but they're an issue in any house with a lower level like this one. Lately, he's found squirrels and voles as well as the odd dormouse in the traps. He takes them out to the woods and releases them, but can't seem to figure out where they get inside."

I nodded. "If they're anything like their North American cousins, they don't need large openings." I raised my chin. "This would've made a great dungeon," I quipped. "There could even have been a torture chamber."

He chuckled. "Possibly, but the house was originally an abbey. The only thing kept down here would've been their wine and brandy. Here you are." He opened the door to the electrical room. "As you can see, it's a mess. The circuits have been bypassed time and again. There's nothing to be done."

I grinned, feeling comfortable and in charge for the first time since leaving Brockton.

"On the contrary, I've dealt with bigger disasters than this. There's plenty of electrical wire here. I should be able to rewire the system and get things back in order in no time. You can go and tell the Baroness that she can stop worrying. By the time the kitchen needs power, they'll have it."

"If you say so," but he sounded skeptical. He turned and left me to it. For the first time since I'd landed in London, I was having fun.

I set the toolbox on the ground, angled the flashlight towards the box, removed the blown fuses, and set to work.

It took me half an hour to trace the wires from the power box to the damaged areas—not chewed by rats as I'd suspected just old and brittle and in need of replacing. I spliced in new wiring, not only where it had broken but at a few other spots that looked as if they might break at any moment, replaced the blown fuses, and turned on the power. The lights came on in the electrical room. After checking a few more circuits and wires, I was satisfied that my job would hold. This place probably needed to be rewired from top to bottom but it would be Montrose's job not mine to convince the Baroness of that. Sweaty, tired, and disheveled, I retraced my steps to the kitchen. The staff was running around getting everything ready.

"Thank the Maker that you were here, lass," the cook said coming over to me. "The Baroness had your things taken up to Lady Melissa's room. I can send one of the girls up to help you. Such a shame that your hair and makeup have been ruined."

"That's okay," I quipped. I figured my hair was full of cobwebs and the Lord alone knew what else, and my face had to be streaked with dirt. "If I can take a shower and clean up, I can repair the damage in no time."

The cook nodded. "Elsie, take her up to Lady Melissa's room. Mind you, use the back stairs. There's no need for any of those who've arrived to see her this way."

The woman was more upset about this than I was. I followed Elsie up the narrow staircase to the specified room.

"Can you get me some towels?"

"Right away, miss.

As soon as she returned with clean towels, I went into the bathroom, stripped off the coveralls and the underwear I would have to don once more, and stepped into the shower. After I'd washed off the grime of a couple of hours of real work, I turned off the water, wrapped myself in a towel, and searched for a hairdryer.

I dried my hair and then pulled it back into a low ponytail, one that would allow the hat to sit on my head. I opened my purse and removed the small container of deodorant I always carried and the tube of lipstick. I found a bottle of sunscreen and used it on my face. No makeup this time, but I was determined to be the best I could be. I put on my underwear, slipped on my dress and wedged sandals, and fixed my hat in place. Finally, I pulled on my gloves. Grabbing my purse, and the pile of wet towels, boots, and coveralls, I went down the back staircase and handed everything to Elsie. Then, back ramrod straight, I went outside through the salon doors.

There were at least two dozen women in the yard sitting at small tables or standing talking. Half of them held wine glasses, a few others what I thought might be lemonade, and several others sipped from dainty china cups.

"There you are, Marissa," the Duchess smiled. She held a wine glass. "Thank you so much for helping out, my dear. What will you have? There's red or white wine, lemonade, or Earl Grey tea."

"For heaven sake, Wiggins," the Baroness said, obviously in her cups. "Bring the girl some champagne. She deserves it. My dear, I don't know how to thank you. You saved the day. I'll be forever grateful."

"My lady, what I've done is only temporary. I suggest you hire an electrical contractor and get the wiring changed as soon as you can. While today's incident was inconvenient, another might cause a fire which would be much worse than a few blown fuses. I'd also consider having someone check the foundation, too."

"I will most definitely do that. As soon as Montrose gets back."

I swallowed my chuckle. By this time tomorrow, she would've forgotten all about it.

Marley came over and hugged me. "Marissa, I don't know what we would've done without you. You're the best. You not only saved her, you saved me. Now, come and meet some of my friends. I want everyone to know what a wonderful big sister I have."

I nodded, buried my hatred of being the center of attention, and arm and arm, we walked through the garden.

* * *

By the time Friday arrived, my face ached from smiling and my head pounded from my attempts at polite if trivial conversation. Remi and his crew arrived in the morning, and I had precious little time to myself. The last few days had been pleasant enough although I'd enjoyed talking to Celia yesterday best of all. She'd heard all about my saving the day at the garden party. It seemed Melissa had pried loose her mother's purse strings and an electrical contractor would start upgrades on the house next week. Celia had also spoken about Ken. She found him fascinating and wanted to know all about him. As my apology to him, I kept my anecdotes to the good things he'd done, but the more I talked about him and Cedar Lake, the more I missed Zak.

Now, I was getting helped into my green gown for the rehearsal. Remi had pulled my hair to the side and curled it for the occasion and the Duchess had lent me a set of diamond earrings and a matching pendant. Ming had painted my toenails and fingernails in the same green as my dress and Sally had done my makeup accordingly.

At six, once more the painted lady, I piled into the Bentley with Mom, the Duchess, Solange, Emily, and Imogene. The others were coming to the village church in separate cars. The more everyone praised the way I looked, the more I missed being able to simply be myself. I understood that in this world, appearances were everything, but I longed for my world where they didn't matter all that much. At one time, Zak had loved me without

375

painted nails, fancy clothes, and makeup. If only I hadn't been so foolish and insecure. I'd thrown away the best thing I'd ever had.

At the church, the minister went over the order in which we would enter. Clara had us all practice the tempo of our steps. The Duke and Duchess would be seated first, then Mom. Once she was, the music would start and the girls would enter first, dropping rose petals from the baskets they carried. I would follow, then Solange, Celia, Louisa Bolt, and the rest of the girls whose names I couldn't recall. Aaron, Jacob, and the other groomsmen would be lined up on the left at the front of the church. Marley would come down the aisle with Dad. Once she reached the front, I would hand my bouquet to Solange and take hers from her, returning it to her and reclaiming mine when the service was complete.

We entered three times before Clara was satisfied. The minister went through the order of service and finally, we returned to the castle for supper. Emily and Imogene were turned over to their nanny and the adults all went into the dining room for dinner. By the time the meal was over, I was praying I could excuse myself and go to bed.

In another three days, I would be returning to Brockton and my life there. In some ways, while I would miss Marley and the friends I'd made here, I would be happy to be back where I felt comfortable. The only thing I would truly pine for was Zak. Somehow I had to find a way to make amends to him. We might never be lovers again, but if we could be friends, it would help.

I would return to England for Christmas with Mom and Dad, but only for a week. This wasn't my life. It might be exciting and fast-paced, but it seemed tedious to me. Marley would excel at charity work and similar activities, while I would molder and die. I needed more from my life than parties, fancy clothes, and the occasional good deed. I needed Zak.

Back at the guest house, I got undressed and ready for bed. I crawled between the sheets and closed my eyes.

The dream started off simply enough. I was running along the road the way I'd done twice since I'd arrived. When I got to the spot where I usually turned around, I couldn't. My legs kept pumping, pulling me deeper and deeper into the forest. The trees crowded the road, blocking out the sunlight.

Suddenly, the road was gone, replaced by a rock-littered path through gnarly trees that had to be thousands of years old. Instead of being firm, hard, and dry, the path was spongy, my feet having difficulty moving, the earth itself wanting to hold me in place. The branches grew longer, not skyward like branches should but toward the ground. The branches turned into arms and hands grabbing at me trying to push me deeper and deeper into the muddy soil. I cried out for help, but the branches covered my mouth. In the background, I saw Zak as caught up and twisted as I was.

"You should've trusted me; I loved you. We could've worked it out," he said before disappearing in a tangle of branches.

I woke, covered in sweat, the sheets and blankets tangled around me, tears running down my cheeks.

I had to go the Cedar Lake. I needed to find Zak and beg him to forgive me, beg him for another chance because without him, I was as lost and tangled in my own misery as I'd been in the nightmare.

* * *

I awoke at six, as tired as I had been when I went to bed. Remi, Ming, and Sally, all worked their magic while I managed to scarf down two cups of coffee. Madame Denis arrived and helped me into my dress, pleased that it needed no adjustments and then went off to help Marley. With the sapphire blue dress, I wore the sapphires and diamond earrings I'd worn the night of the masquerade. Once I was dressed, Remi returned to add a thin sapphire and diamond headband to my hair.

At the church, Clara handed out the bouquets, consisting of three types of British-grown orchids: white cattleya, odontoglossum, and cypripedium, the same flowers that had been part of Queen Elizabeth's bouquet when she'd married Prince Phillip.

Other than Imogene having to go to the bathroom at the last second, Emily running out of rose petals before she got to the front, and Celia wanting her mother rather loudly in the church, the wedding had gone off smoothly. The luncheon at the church hall had been well-attended by all the people who were of the Duke of Habersham's Duchy, the counties which were his responsibility. Now, with the rest of the Sykes family occupied, I had a couple of hours to myself before Remi, Ming, and Sally would be back to get me ready for the evening's wedding supper and dance.

I glanced out the window. There were several couples walking in the yard taking advantage of the lovely weather. There was a tent full of drinks and food for the guest staying at the castle, but unlike

Celia and the others, I didn't want to mix anymore. I needed "me" time.

The sound of a car engine had me looking left as a taxi came down the lane. No doubt one of the supper guests was arriving early. I debated going out for a run, but the vestiges of the nightmare kept me from doing so. Finally, unable to sit here and do nothing, I put on my jeans and a t-shirt, one of the few normal outfits I'd packed, and giving the wedding guests a large berth, I went over to the stables. I'd meant to visit them earlier, but there simply hadn't been time.

I leaned against the corral fence watching the beautiful animals grazing there. Were the ones Zak had accompanied from Canada here?

"Hello, Marissa."

I turned at the sound of Zak's voice. His eyes were shadowed and he looked as if he hadn't slept in days, but he was the most beautiful thing I'd ever seen. Tears brimmed my eyes.

"You're back .. I—"

Before I could finish what I was going to say, he pulled me into his arms and kissed me.

The ouch and texture of his lips were familiar and I responded like a staving woman finally tossed a crust of bread. When he licked my lips, I opened to him eagerly, and the sweet sensation and taste I'd missed these last five years flooded me. I responded to his embrace with everything in me, hoping he could feel my love as well as my regret for what I'd done to him, to us. I didn't want the kiss to stop. As long as we were clenched to one another like this, there was a chance we could fix what had been broken.

CHAPTER FIFTEEN

I don't know how long we stood there in each other's arms, our mouths melded together, but slowly he pulled away, leaning his forehead against mine.

"You have no idea how long I've wanted to do that." He smiled at me. "It's nice to see you looking the way I remember you. I never thought I was good enough for you five years ago, and seeing you with all the royalty, looking so beautiful, regal, and way out of my league ... is it okay to say I prefer you like this? Like my Marissa."

I gazed into his gray eyes, mine filled with tears.

"But you left."

He frowned. "I had to go. I was always going back to Canada for a couple of days. Aaron knew that."

"But I didn't. Oh, God. When Marley told me you'd left..." The tears slid down my cheeks. "I'm so sorry. I shouldn't have destroyed my phone. I shouldn't have stayed away. I loved you so much and I was so hurt and angry, but not at you, at me for losing to Karen when I needed to win the most. And then to find out that you could've drowned..."

By now the tears were running freely down my cheeks.

"Shh! It wasn't all your fault. First things first. I didn't leave because of what Karen said. I was mad, yes, and I needed time to think things through, but I really did have to get back to Canada to attend to a business matter. Just as I was getting ready to go, some idiot left the gate open between Jack Frenhouse's cattle field and the neighboring alfalfa field. His animals got in there and as expected, the Jerseys' got bloat."

"Oh, no! How many?" As a farmer's daughter, I knew how dangerous bloat could be if left untreated.

"More than a hundred head. It took every vet in the area, including myself, to treat them all in time before we lost any of them. I missed my flight back, but I couldn't get another one right away. But all that time at the airport gave me time to dig deep inside myself. I went over every single aspect of that day. The one thing that stuck in my head was my willingness to believe we'd had a fight and you'd broken off our engagement. It came to me that I'd expected you to do just that, not because we weren't in love, but because I was holding you back. There was no way you would ever own your own electrical repair company in Cedar Lake and we both knew it. Joe Rasmussen and his sons would never sell. You could work for him for twenty years and never get ahead."

"It wouldn't have mattered." But it had and I'd been lying to myself for years about it. I'd wanted to leave the area and relocate elsewhere, but Zak loved Cedar Lake.

"Marissa, that's a lie and you know it, but it's taken me five years to realize that it isn't the place that's important; it's the people there with you."

I sniffled, about to confess that I would gladly give up my business and go back to doing menial jobs for Joe and his son just to be with him.

"I found out you were in Brockton just after Ken had his accident. Your Aunt Yvette thought someone should tell you if Ken died."

I gasped. "Why didn't you call?"

"Because he didn't die. I was curious and looked you up on the Internet. As a licensed electrician, you were registered. I kept stalking the site and found out you'd bought *Power and Light*. You had your own business, just like you wanted, but you were more than twenty-five hundred miles away from me, not exactly commuting distance. I talked to your mother, but she wouldn't say much beyond the fact that you were doing well and had no plans to come back to Cedar Lake. I convinced myself that you were better off without me."

"I wasn't. I'm not. I—"

"Let me finish, please?"

I nodded.

"When Aaron bought the ranch, he hadn't met your sister yet. He talked about his fiancée, but it wasn't until a few weeks later that he mentioned she'd been born in Cedar Lake. When I realized it was Marley, I started wondering about you. I never stopped loving you and missing you, but since I couldn't be sure why we'd argued ... A few months ago, Ken came to the clinic and offered me your engagement ring. He explained where he'd found it and while I didn't recall being in the hot tub, it did explain why I'd been naked in the morning. That clinched it for me. The fight must've been over your hopes and dreams and my dogged refusal to consider leaving Cedar Lake and the clinic. If I wanted to give us a second chance I had to find a way to see you in person. When Aaron asked me to escort the horses in England, I discovered you were going to be the Maid of Honor. If I was going to try to make this work, I had one chance and only one ... I wrangled an invitation to the opera and the masquerade ball as well as the wedding. I was sure that if only I could just talk to you, make you understand that I would do whatever it took to try to make things work between us, but you were adamant that we had nothing to talk about ... I wasn't expecting Karen and Ken to be there." He shrugged. "When I saw you again, looking so damn gorgeous, I realized what an ass I'd been. If I'd swallowed my pride and had gone to you in Brockton, begged you to forgive me for whatever I'd done..."

"Stop." I held my hand over his lips. "There's nothing to forgive. You did nothing wrong. I have to confess something. The night of the masquerade, I was in the garden—you know when I disappeared." I related what I'd overheard and what Matt had said. "Maybe he was right. Maybe I was looking for an excuse to get away. I felt smothered, not by you but by my mother's expectations that I would give up the silly notion of being an electrician and settle down, by always having Ken and Karen in my life, and by my fear that everyone was right, and I would fail. But it doesn't matter now. I'll be an electrician no matter where I am. I've proven myself. Why I even did some work here. I've missed Cedar Lake and the mountains, but most of all I've missed you. I know we can't go back and what was said can't be unsaid, but can we at least be friends? We used to be the best of friends."

Zak shook his head. "No. I want more than friendship, Rissa, I want you in my life as my lover, my wife, my partner. I won't live without you. I can't. I made a few calls before coming to London with the horses. There's an opening for a large animal veterinarian in Brockton. I sold my practice in Cedar Lake to Cal Winters, a friend from Calgary who was looking to find a job working with livestock. He's one of the best when it comes to horses, having grown up on a ranch in Montana. That's why I had to go back this week. I signed the papers while I was there. I start in Brockton in two weeks."

I could hardly believe what I was hearing.

"You did all that before you even saw me again? What if I were engaged or married?"

"You weren't. Marley has been giving me updates ever since I found out about the wedding. She's a real romantic and was sure that with the right staging, I could win your heart again. I just needed the right opportunity. Karen's confession threw me for a loop because I thought I was making progress, and then all of a sudden I was back to square one, and angry because I thought Ken had taken you away from me. What happened five years ago doesn't matter. We both made mistakes. What matters now is that I love you and I want to be with you. Tell me you feel the same way. Tell me you'll marry me."

Instead of speaking, I stood on my tiptoes and kissed him.

* * *

When I stepped into the ballroom on Zak's arm, that night, My hair styled in a smooth chignon, my makeup subtle, and the red dress showing off all my curves, in addition to the diamond earrings Aaron had given me as a thank you gift, I wore my platinum engagement ring.

"Marissa, you're absolutely, glowing child," the Duchess said. "I'm happy for you."

"I'm happy for me, too, Your Grace. I came here to be Marley's Maid of Honor. I'm going home to be Zak's wife. It's a Match I've always dreamed of."

Zak smiled. "Definitely, and I believe this is your drink." He pointed to the cocktail coupe of the tray the server held.

"Yup, the best two matches ever made." I smiled. This was definitely the most fun I'd had in ages.

Afterword

I hope you enjoyed **It's a Match**. If so, please take a few minutes to leave an honest review on Amazon. Authors enjoy hearing that readers like their stories. There is no better promotion for an author than word of mouth from a satisfied reader.

My website has a list of all of my books if you want to read another of my works. https://mhsusannematthews.ca/

Thanks again,

Stay safe,

Susanne

ABOUT THE AUTHOR

Susanne Matthews was born and raised in Eastern Ontario, Canada. She is of French-Canadian descent. She's always been an avid reader of all types of books, but with a penchant for happily ever after romances. A retired educator, Susanne spends her time writing and creating adventures for her readers. She loves the ins and outs of romance, and the complex journey it takes to get from the first word to the last period of a novel. As she writes, her characters take on a life of their own, and she shares their fears and agonies on the road to self-discovery and love.

Website: http://www.mhsusannematthews.ca/
Blog:https://wordpress.com/view/livingthedream941447545.wordpress.com
Facebook: https://www.facebook.com/SLMauthor
Author Amazon:
https://www.amazon.com/Susanne-Matthews/e/B00DJCKRP4
Goodreads:
https://www.goodreads.com/author/show/7009276.Susanne_Matthews
Twitter: @jandsmatt

Novels By Susanne Matthews

Suspense/thrillers:

The Harvester Files
The White Carnation, Book One
The White Lily, Book Two
The White Iris Book Three
The White Dahlia Book Four

Vengeance Is Mine Series:
On His Watch, Book One
Fire Angel, Book Two
In Plain Sight, Book Three
No Good Deed, Book Four
Secrets and Lies, Book Five

Paranormal
Mythic Adventures
Echoes of the Past
Hello Again
Atonement

Timeless Love
Beneath the Ashes

Paranormal Series: The Punishers
The Tigress, Book One
The Guardian, Book Two

Other Suspense:
Sworn to Protect
Desert Deception
All For Love (Christian)
Prove It! (YA)

HISTORICAL

The Captain's Promise
The Price of Honor, Canadiana Series, Book One
The Price of Courage (Canadiana Series, Book Two)
Twist of Fate The Golden Legacy

CONTEMPORARY ROMANCE:
All For Love:
Just For The Weekend
Forever and Always
Wedding Bell Blues
The Blue Dragon
Same Time Next Year (Women's Fiction)
The Regal Rose
Royal Flush
Trouble With Eden
Finding Melinda

Cocktails for You Series
Tequila Sunrise, Book One
Champagne Cocktail, Book Two
Buck's Fizz
The Tipsy Pig
Make Mine a Manhattan
Emerald Glow
Sea Breeze
It's a Match

Christmas Books
Holiday Magic (Christmas)
The Perfect Choice (Christmas)
Come Home for Christmas (Christmas)
Forever in my Heart
His Christmas Family
Murder & Mistletoe

Made in United States
North Haven, CT
06 June 2025

69551423R00222